Miracles at Muswell Hill Hospital

Christmas is a time for healing broken hearts!

Medical marvels occur every day
at Muswell Hill Hospital—but two friends
who work there, Dr Hayley Clark and
Dr Danielle (Dani) Owens, are deserving of
some special Christmas miracles. Bonded by recent
traumatic life events, they've helped
each other recover with their year-long pact
of saying yes to everything!

As Christmas draws near—ready or not—
they are about to meet two gorgeous guys
who, if they will just let them in,
can finally mend their broken hearts!

Hayley and Sam's story
Christmas with Her Daredevil Doc

Sam and Hayley had one incredible week in
Iceland—but when Sam appears for work at
Muswell Hill Hospital, they struggle to keep their
'temporary' romance in the past. Can their holiday
fling become so much more?

And Dani and Alex's story
Their Pregnancy Gift

Alex is determined never to have children—
but Danielle is irresistible. And after one
night of passion they must face the shocking
and wonderful consequences!

Both available now!

Dear Reader,

How would you react if you discovered that your entire life had been based on a lie, and you weren't who you'd always thought you were? That's what Alex, my hero, has to contend with. Worse still, there's a fifty-fifty chance that he's inherited an incurable genetic disease.

Enter Dani, my heroine—whose ex *really* let her down. Along with her best friend, she's agreed to a 'Year of Saying Yes'—agreeing to opportunities that will make her life better. As part of that she comforts Alex when his life takes another nosedive, and it results in something that could mean absolute disaster or total happiness.

Which way will they go? I hope you enjoy their journey of discovery.

With love,

Kate Hardy

THEIR PREGNANCY GIFT

BY
KATE HARDY

MILLS
BOON

Published in Great Britain 2017
By Mills & Boon, an imprint of HarperCollins*Publishers*
1 London Bridge Street, London, SE1 9GF

© 2017 Pamela Brooks

ISBN: 978-0-263-07018-7

MIX
Paper from
responsible sources
FSC® C007454

This book is produced from independently certified FSC paper
to ensure responsible forest management. For more information
visit www.harpercollins.co.uk/green.

Printed and bound in Great Britain
by CPI Group (UK) Ltd, Croydon, CR0 4YY

Kate Hardy has always loved books, and could read before she went to school. She discovered Mills & Boon books when she was twelve and decided this was what she wanted to do. When she isn't writing Kate enjoys reading, cinema, ballroom dancing and the gym. You can contact her via her website: katehardy.com.

Books by Kate Hardy

Mills & Boon Medical Romance

Paddington Children's Hospital

Mummy, Nurse…Duchess?

Christmas Miracles in Maternity

The Midwife's Pregnancy Miracle

Her Playboy's Proposal
Capturing the Single Dad's Heart

Mills & Boon Cherish

Holiday with the Best Man
Falling for the Secret Millionaire
Her Festive Doorstep Baby

Visit the Author Profile page
at millsandboon.co.uk for more titles.

To Tony and Debbie, with much love.

CHAPTER ONE

'I CAN'T WAIT to get rid of you,' Danielle said. 'You've made me miserable, you've stopped me doing everything I love doing, and I do actually *hate* you.'

She looked up to see Alex, the new consultant on the maternity ward, standing in the open doorway of her office.

He raised an eyebrow. 'Practising your break-up speech?'

Dani felt the colour flood into her face. 'I hope I'd be a little kinder than that.' Certainly kinder than Leo had been to her, last Christmas Eve, when he'd told her that their marriage was over and he was leaving her for someone else. Someone else who was expecting his baby—when he'd told Dani only a few months before that he wasn't ready to start a family.

She pushed the thought away. 'If you must know, I was talking to my walking cast.'

'Right.'

There wasn't even the glimmer of a smile, and she sighed inwardly. From what she'd seen of him over the last couple of months, Alex Morgan was good with their patients, but all his social skills seemed to switch off as soon as he had to deal with his colleagues on anything other than a work basis. He hadn't been to a single team night out, always ate lunch on his own, and if he was in the staff kitchen he never joined in with the conversation.

She didn't think he was being snooty; but she didn't think he was shy, either. There was obviously a reason why he kept his distance from everyone else, but Dani—who'd always got on well with everyone—had no idea how to reach him. He was possibly the most difficult person in the department to have as the co-organiser of the ward's Christmas party, but she'd just have to make the best of it.

'You wanted to see me?' he asked.

'We need to talk about organising the ward's Christmas meal. Are you busy at lunchtime today, or can we discuss it over a sandwich?'

'Sorry. I have meetings,' he said.

Dani didn't believe a word of it, but the ward's Christmas meal still needed to be sorted out. If she gave Alex a longer timeframe, he'd be forced to pick a day. And if he picked one of the two evenings this week when she was busy, then she'd move her other arrangements because she really wanted to get this done and dusted. She gave him the sweetest, sweetest smile. 'OK. Do you have time for a coffee after work some time in the next two weeks to discuss it?'

He masked his expression quickly, but not before Dani had seen it. He'd obviously realised what her game plan was, and he couldn't think of a decent excuse that would work for two whole weeks.

Gotcha, she thought in satisfaction.

He took his phone out of his pocket and made a show of checking his diary, though she was pretty sure it wasn't that full.

'How about tomorrow?' he suggested.

'That'll be fine, as Hayley's training with Sam tomorrow night.' She glared at her cast. 'Thanks to this.'

'Uh-huh.'

OK. So he wasn't going to bite. Anyone else would've been polite enough to ask what she'd done to her foot, or at least make a comment. But Alex clearly didn't want to get into conversation with her. Fair enough. She couldn't force him to make friends with her. If he wanted to keep himself to himself, that was his decision and it wasn't her place to try and change it.

'Thank you. I'll meet you outside the staffroom tomorrow after our shift,' she said.

'Fine,' he said.

And still he didn't give her a single smile.

She sighed inwardly, and got on with writing up the case notes from her clinic that morning.

God, what was wrong with him? Alex wondered as he headed to his own office. Danielle Owens was *nice.* She'd been friendly right from his first day on the ward, trying to make him feel part of the team, and in response he'd been completely standoffish. Meeting her for a drink tomorrow night to discuss the team's Christmas meal was the only social invitation he'd accepted in the two months he'd been working at Muswell Hill Memorial Hospital, and that was solely because the head of the department had blithely informed him that his predecessor had been scheduled to organise it with Dani and he was sure that Alex would be happy to step into those shoes, too.

Actually, Alex wasn't happy about it. At all. But he didn't have much choice.

Maybe he should've taken a longer break. But six

months was surely long enough to get your head round
the fact that you weren't who you thought you were, and
everything you'd always believed wasn't true. He needed
to stop sulking about it and just get on with things. And
he'd really missed his job. At least he knew who he was
at work. Alexander Morgan, obstetric consultant.

He shook himself. Now wasn't the time to start brooding. Or to wonder whether his shortness of temper and
foul mood was an early sign of the incurable neurodegenerative disease that the man he now had to think of
as his father was suffering from. He had notes to write
up, a sandwich to eat, and a clinic to sort out.

'OK, Mrs Hamilton—may I call you Judy?' Dani asked.

The other woman nodded, looking wretched.

'According to our notes, you're sixteen weeks pregnant at the moment, and your midwife asked if I could
fit you into my clinic today.'

Judy dragged in a breath. 'Thank you so much for seeing me, Dr Owens.'

'Call me Dani. And it's no problem. So tell me how
things are going,' Dani said.

'It's awful,' Judy said. 'I've never felt so ill in my entire life. I can't keep anything down, even water. I've
tried everything—sniffing lemons, drinking ginger tea
and eating a dry biscuit before I get up in the morning.
I'm not doing any cooking, and when I do try to eat it's
things that don't smell and are high in carbs and not fatty,
but I still can't keep anything down.'

Judy was doing all the right things to help with morning sickness, Dani knew; but what she was suffering
from sounded rather more serious than everyday morning sickness.

'Nothing works, and all I seem to do is throw up all day.' Judy grimaced. 'My boss sent me home from work today, saying I had to take a few days off, and there was blood in the vomit last time I threw up. That's why I called my midwife, because I was so worried.'

'I'm glad you did. Did the blood look like little streaks?' Dani asked.

Judy nodded.

'OK. I know it looks scary but it's actually quite normal in pregnancy,' Dani reassured her. 'When you've been sick a lot, the lining of your oesophagus gets irritated and it's more likely to get a tiny little tear in it, which is why you saw blood. But we really need to get to the bottom of why you're being sick all the time. Are you OK for me to take a blood sample from you?'

Judy looked slightly nervous. 'I hate needles, but yes.'

Dani took a sample of blood to check Judy's electrolytes, renal function and liver function.

'And can I ask you to get on the scales for me?' She checked the display. 'You've lost four kilograms since your last check-up.'

'Is that bad?'

'It's completely what I expected, with what you've told me about being so sick,' Dani said, and handed Judy a sample bottle. 'Can you do me a midstream urine sample, please?'

While Judy was in the toilet, Dani sent the blood tests off. When Judy came back, the urine sample was quite dark, indicating that Judy was dehydrated, and a dipstick test showed signs of ketones, where the body broke down fat instead of glucose for energy.

'Is it all OK?' Judy asked.

'All your symptoms added together are giving me

a better picture,' Dani said. She checked Judy's notes. 'When you had your twelve-week scan, the radiographer confirmed there was only one baby.' And, to Dani's relief, there was also no indication of a molar pregnancy.

'And then I was sick on the bed,' Judy said miserably. 'Everyone I know says morning sickness goes by twelve weeks, but that was a month ago for me. I feel worse every day, instead of better.'

'Morning sickness can last for up to twenty weeks,' Dani said, 'but in your case I agree with your midwife. I think you have hyperemesis gravidarum—which is a very severe form of morning sickness.'

'Did I do something wrong to get it?' Judy asked.

'No. We don't actually know what causes it, though it does seem to run in families. Do you know if your mum had it, or do you have a sister who had it?'

Judy shook her head. 'Mum never said, and I'm an only child.'

'The most likely cause is hormonal activity, which I know doesn't help you much,' Dani said.

'I feel rotten, but I can live with that as long as the baby's all right.' Judy bit her lip. 'Though I can't eat anything, so I'm scared the baby's not getting proper nutrition.'

'Try not to worry,' Dani said, and squeezed her hand. 'It's very possible that the baby will be smaller than average because of your situation, but we'll keep a close eye on you. I hope it reassures you to know that being sick isn't going to hurt your baby—though obviously it's very miserable for you.'

'I can't believe how bad all kinds of things smell, even tins. I can't stand being on the Tube because of the smell of people's armpits—and it must be so much worse in summer.' Judy shuddered at the thought, and retched again.

Dani handed her a tissue. 'I'm going to admit you to the ward and put you on a drip so we can get some fluids into you,' she said. 'We can also give you some medicine that will help to stop the sickness.'

Judy frowned. 'But won't that harm my baby?'

'No. We'll give you some tablets that are safe for the baby,' Dani reassured her. 'You'll be able to take them at home as well.'

Judy closed her eyes for a moment. 'I'm so tired. I don't think I can cope with this for much longer.'

'Hyperemesis can last for a long time, and I have to tell you that in some cases it doesn't actually get better until the baby arrives,' Dani warned.

'So I might be sick like this for the rest of my pregnancy?'

'Hopefully not. Let's see how you're feeling after a day or so in here,' Dani said. 'Once you're no longer dehydrated, you've had some proper rest and maybe managed to keep something down, you'll feel a bit better.'

'So I have to stay in?'

Dani nodded. 'For a day or two, so we can keep an eye on you. And, because we want you on bed rest, we'll get you to wear compression stockings and give you some heparin injections, to make sure you don't develop any blood clots. I'll have a word with your consultant at the end of my clinic, and he might come and have a chat with you. But in the meantime I'll get one of the midwives to help settle you onto the ward. Is there someone we can call for you?'

'My husband,' Judy said.

Dani checked his mobile number with Judy. 'I'll call him while you're getting settled on the ward, and maybe he can bring you some things from home.'

'Thank you.' Judy's eyes filled with tears. 'I feel so stupid, making such a fuss.'

'You're not making a fuss,' Dani said. 'You have a medical condition that's making you feel awful, and my job's to help you feel better. You did exactly the right thing, calling your midwife—and your midwife did the right thing, telling you to come here.' She opened the door of the consulting room and went over to the first midwife she could see. 'Jas, I've got a mum with hyper-emesis and I want her admitted to the ward and put on a drip. Would you be able to settle her in for me, please?'

'Sure,' Jas said with a smile.

'Thanks.'

Back in the consulting room, Dani introduced Jas to Judy. 'Judy, this is Jasminder Lund, one of our midwives. Jas, this is Judy Hamilton. Judy, Jas is going to look after you, and I'll pop in and see you after my clinic.'

'Thank you so much,' Judy said, and let Jas lead her out to the ward.

Dani called Judy's husband and explained what was happening, and then checked Judy's file to see who her consultant was. Hopefully it would be Anton Powell; he was always really good with worried mums.

The file said otherwise and she sighed inwardly. Oh, great. It *would* have to be Alex Morgan. But Dani would just have to sideline her impatience with him, because Judy and the baby's welfare came first.

She saw the rest of the mums on her list, then went to find Alex in his office.

'Do you have a moment, please?' she asked. 'I need to talk to you about one of your patients.'

'Sure.' His voice was carefully neutral, and so was his expression.

'Judy Hamilton. She's dehydrated, losing weight, her urine showed ketones, and I'm waiting for her bloods to come back.' Dani swiftly ran through the case with him. 'I've admitted her with hyperemesis, and asked Jas to settle her in and put her on a drip.'

'Good call,' he said.

'I told her I'd talk to you at the end of my clinic, then go and see her.'

'I'll come with you,' he said.

On the way to Judy's room, he collected a cup of ice chips.

When they walked in, Judy was retching miserably into a bowl. Without a word—and before Dani could do it herself—Alex found a cloth and moistened it. When Judy had finished being sick, he wiped her face gently, and handed her the cup of ice chips. 'I know right now you can't keep anything down, but you might find that sucking on an ice chip will make your mouth feel a little better,' he said. 'Hello, Mrs Hamilton. I'm Alex Morgan, your consultant, and Dani here's told me how terrible you're feeling.'

'I'm sor—' she began.

'There's nothing to apologise for,' he cut in, 'so please don't worry. Hyperemesis is a medical condition that unfortunately affects some women, and right now I'm guessing you're really tired, really unhappy and feeling absolutely terrible.'

She nodded, and brushed away a tear.

He smiled at her. 'The good news is that we can help

you. I know Dani's already explained that we've put you on a drip to rehydrate you, and we can give you some medication to help with the sickness. It won't hurt the baby and we'll keep a very close eye on you so we can make you more comfortable.'

Dani was stunned by that smile. It lit up his face, and Alex's blue-green eyes were amazing. When he smiled, he was probably the most gorgeous man in the entire hospital. But she damped down the attraction as soon as it flared. This was so inappropriate, it was untrue. Apart from the fact that he was her senior on the ward, she was pretty sure he didn't like her, and she wasn't wasting any more of her emotions on men who couldn't or wouldn't love her back.

But if Alex could be as charming as this with their mums, why couldn't he be like this with the rest of the staff? He'd have everyone eating out of his hand instead of feeling as if they were treading on eggshells around him. Though he had at least agreed to meet her tomorrow and discuss the ward's Christmas meal. Maybe she could turn that planned coffee after work into dinner, and get him to be a little more receptive to changing his attitude at work.

'If you're worried about anything at all, we're all here to help,' Alex continued. 'The midwives here are a great bunch and really know their stuff, and the doctors are all really approachable.'

Dani stored that one away to tell them, because she was pretty sure Alex hadn't told them that himself.

'And remember, no question is ever silly. You won't be the first to ask it and you won't be the last. We'd all much rather you asked than sat there worrying,' Dani said, and squeezed Judy's hand briefly in reassurance.

'I called your husband, and he's going to bring in some clothes and toiletries for you straight after work.'

'Thank you,' Judy said, a tear leaking down her face.

It wasn't the first time Alex had worked with Dani, but he'd forgotten how lovely she was with their mums—patient, kind and reassuring.

Though it wasn't just her manner at work that attracted him. It was her energy, the brightness of her dark eyes and her smile. In another life, he would have asked her out on the first day he'd met her.

But he wasn't in a position where he could consider starting a relationship, or even having a simple friendship with someone. Not until he'd sorted his head out.

He was going to have to be very careful. Because he had a nasty feeling that Danielle Owens could be very dangerous to his peace of mind.

CHAPTER TWO

'DARLING? SAD NEWS, I'm afraid. Stephen died last night.'

Alex replayed his mother's message on his voicemail for the tenth time. It still hadn't quite sunk in. Stephen was dead. *His father was dead.* At the rather less than ripe old age of fifty-seven.

So if Alex had inherited the faulty gene and he followed Stephen's pattern, that meant he had twenty-two years of life left—the last five years of which really wouldn't be worth living.

He swallowed hard. It was an 'if', admittedly, but there was still a fifty per cent chance that he had the gene. Scary odds. The simple toss of a coin.

He picked up the phone to call his parents, but then put it down again. What could he say? How could you really be sorry for the death of someone you barely knew, had met twice and who had never really acknowledged you as his child? It'd be just a platitude. Meaningless. And his relationship with his parents had been seriously strained since his mother had dropped the bombshell eight months ago that his father wasn't actually his father, and his biological father had advanced Huntington's disease. Right now Alex wasn't in the mood for polite awkwardness,

and he didn't want to make the situation worse by accidentally saying something wrong.

And there was nobody—absolutely nobody—he could
talk to about this. He was an only child; and he'd dis-
tanced himself from everyone in his life since learning the news. He'd broken his engagement to Lara, and
avoided all his friends, even his best friend Tom, until
they'd got the message and stopped calling him. So being
alone now was completely his own fault: but, on the other
hand, how could he have been unfair enough to dump
his worries on any of them?

*My dad isn't actually my dad, and my 'real' dad—who
I've never met—might have passed on a genetic disease
that'll leave me a drooling, shambling wreck when I'm
only in my fifties.*

How could he possibly have married Lara, knowing
that she would end up having to be his carer rather than
his partner? How could he have denied her the chance to
have children, too—because, if he had the faulty gene,
there was a fifty per cent chance of passing that same
gene on to his children and condemning them to an ill-
ness that still had no cure?

Lara had clearly thought the same, because Alex had
seen a very different side of her when he'd told her the
news. Of course she'd been sympathetic when the bombshell had first dropped—but he'd noticed her backing
away a little more each day, once they'd looked up the
symptoms of Huntington's and seen what the end stage
was like.

She hadn't wanted to come to America with him, either, saying she was too busy at work—but he'd seen the
real reason in her eyes. She was afraid of facing what
might be ahead for them. Alex hadn't wanted her to stay

with him out of duty, especially once he'd seen the burden that Stephen's partner Catriona carried. But he knew that if Lara broke their engagement, people would judge her harshly and see her as the woman who hadn't been prepared to stand by her man. That wasn't fair, because Huntington's was a horrible disease and it would be a massive burden. So he'd done the right thing by both of them and ended it. And it had underlined for him that he'd be spending the rest of his life on his own. It wasn't fair to ask someone to share a future that could be so, so difficult.

He'd heard through the grapevine that Lara had met someone else. He hoped her new partner would give her the shiny, hopeful future he hadn't been able to promise her. Though right now his own hopes of a shiny, hopeful future had just taken another battering.

The only thing he could do was head for the gym and push himself in the weights room until he was too physically exhausted to think. And please let tomorrow be a better day.

Danielle was half tempted to throw her glass of water over Alex Morgan. For pity's sake. He'd agreed to meet her to sort out the ward's Christmas meal. It shouldn't take too long. Surely he could manage his dislike of her for that short a time and actually pay attention to what she needed to discuss with him?

But just for a moment there was something in his expression. As if he'd been sucked into a black hole and there was no way out.

Maybe this wasn't about him not wanting to deal with her.

Her fixer instincts kicked in. 'Are you all right?' she asked.

Sheer panic flashed over his face and was swiftly hidden before he drawled, 'Why do you ask?'

'Because,' she said, 'I've asked you the same question three times now and you still haven't replied.'

'It's been a busy day,' he said.

'About the same as mine.' Maybe it really was that simple, after all, and she was just making excuses for him. The guy didn't like her and wasn't even bothering to hide it. And she'd had enough. It was time to face this head on and sort it out. 'Look, do you have a problem working with me? Have I done something to upset you?'

He looked surprised. 'No, nothing like that.'

Seriously? Did he not know he behaved as if she was the horrible child who'd had a screaming tantrum and popped all the balloons at his birthday party before stamping on his presents and tipping his cake onto the floor?

Or maybe he was one of those bright but emotionally clueless men and he didn't mean anything by his behaviour after all. OK. This was her cue to change the subject and talk about the Christmas meal again. Except she remembered that look of utter devastation in his eyes and it made her decide to take a risk. She chose her words carefully. 'Alex, I know you don't really socialise with the team, and it's absolutely none of my business why you choose not to, but right now you seem really unhappy and as if you could do with a friend.'

That was an understatement.

Except Alex had chosen to push his friends away. Just as he'd chosen to make sure he kept all interactions with his colleagues strictly professional since he'd started at Muswell Hill Hospital.

'Just so you know,' Dani said, 'I'm not a gossip. Anything you decide to tell me will stay with me.'

It was tempting to confide in her. So very, very tempting. Her warmth and kindness drew him.

In other circumstances, Alex would've already asked Dani out. He liked the way she was at work, friendly and kind with everyone, reassuring their patients and giving the junior staff a chance to boost their experience and shine. Not to mention that she was gorgeous. A pocket Venus, with that glorious dark hair she kept tied back at work, dark eyes that seemed to understand everything, and a perfect rosebud mouth that made him want to kiss her.

But he couldn't get involved with anyone. Not now. Not with that ticking time bomb hanging over him. It wouldn't be fair.

'I...' He searched for an excuse, but the words just wouldn't come.

'OK. This is what we're going to do. We're going to eat carbs,' she said softly, 'in a quiet place where nobody can overhear us.'

He couldn't quite process what she meant, because his head was all over the place.

As if she'd guessed, she said, 'We'll get a pizza delivered to my place. Which isn't a come-on.'

Pizza. Her place. He blinked. 'Won't your partner mind?'

'I've been divorced officially since the summer. Which doesn't mean that I'm desperate to replace my ex and get married again, if that's a concern for you.' She paused. 'I should ask you the same. Will your partner mind?'

'No partner.' He'd broken off his engagement to Lara the day after he'd come back to England from America.

'That's settled, then.' She gathered up the papers she'd spread in front of her and put them back into the cardboard wallet file. 'Let's go.'

Enough of his brain cells still worked to make him ask, 'Is it far? Should you be walking anywhere with that thing on your foot?'

She smiled, as if pleased that he'd remembered about her foot. 'It's not that far and yes—that's why it's called a walking cast. Trust me, I'm not doing anything that will set back the date when I can get rid of this thing. I'm counting down the days.'

He was aware he'd never actually asked her about it—which was pretty rude of him. Being polite to his colleagues didn't mean getting close to them. 'What did you do?'

'Stress fracture. Second and third metatarsal.' She rolled her eyes. 'Probably caused by my new running shoes. Which are *so* being replaced when I can run again. Unfortunately, that'll be after physio and well after the charity run is held, but my best friend is the most wonderful woman in the world and she talked the event organisers into letting her run in my place. We're raising money for the new baby-sized MRI scanner for the ward,' she explained.

'Put me down for sponsorship.'

She smiled. 'There's no need. That wasn't a hint. And I talk too much. Right. Pizza. What do you like?'

He couldn't think straight. 'Anything.'

'Is there anything you hate? Olives? Anchovies?'

He grimaced. 'Not anchovies, please.'

'Let's keep it simple, then. Margherita pizza and dough balls,' she said. 'And I have salad in the fridge. So we're sorted.'

Before Alex could even offer to pay, she'd already called the order through and was shepherding him out of the door of the café.

As they walked back to her place, he was relieved that she didn't push him to talk. She didn't chatter on about nothing, either; she was surprisingly easy to be with. And oh, God, it was good not to feel quite so alone. That phone message last night had felt as if the axe hanging over him had taken a practice swipe a little too close to the top of his head.

She unlocked the door to her flat and ushered him inside. 'OK. I can offer you three types of tea, very strong coffee, a glass of water or a glass of wine.'

When Alex couldn't gather his thoughts enough to respond, she said, 'I'll be bossy and choose. Wine it is. Hope you don't mind white.'

'It's fine, thank you.'

This was what he'd admired about her on the ward. The way she saw what needed to be done and got on with it, sorting things out without a fuss. She was a bit on the bossy side, perhaps, but her smile took the sting out of that. She had a good heart. Enormous. Look at the way she was being so kind to him right now, when he'd been surly and was an utter mess.

She took a bottle from the fridge and poured him a glass of wine. Then she set the table and put a salad together.

When the pizza and dough balls arrived, he stared at her in dismay. 'Sorry. I've been so rude.' The least he could've done was offer to help lay the table. Instead, he'd just sat there and stared into his glass.

'Don't apologise and don't worry about it. Eat your pizza and drink your wine,' she said.

So she wasn't going to make him talk?

Relief flooded through him. Part of him wanted to talk, to let all the poison out; but part of him still wanted to lock everything away, the way he had for the last few months.

They ate their meal in silence, but it wasn't awkward. Alex felt weirdly comfortable with her; and at the same time that feeling of comfortableness unsettled him. He knew Dani on a professional level, but they weren't friends. Shouldn't this feel strained or, at the very least, slightly awkward? But right now he felt as if he'd known Danielle Owens for ever.

What was a little more worrying was the way every nerve end tingled with awareness when his hand accidentally brushed against hers as they reached for the dough balls at the same time. In another world, another life, this meal would've been so different. The start of something, full of anticipation and possibilities.

But he was a mess and she was being far kinder to him than he deserved, after being so standoffish and difficult at work.

She topped up his glass without comment, and he had just about enough presence of mind to grab a tea towel when she washed up their plates.

And then she shepherded him through to the living room.

'All righty,' she said. 'You look as if you were in pretty much the same place as I was, last Christmas. I was lucky because my best friend dragged me out and made me talk. So I'm paying it forward and being the person who makes you talk. Spill.'

Talk. How on earth could he put the mess of his life

into words? Alex looked at her. 'I don't even know where to start.'

She shrugged. 'Anywhere. Just talk. I'm not going to judge and I'm not going to tell anyone else what you tell me.'

This was his cue to refuse politely and leave. But, to his horror, instead the words started spilling out and they just wouldn't stop.

'It started eight months ago. My mum asked me to meet her for lunch. And then she told me my dad wasn't my dad. I'd grown up believing I was one person, and then suddenly I wasn't who I thought I was.'

She said nothing, but reached over to squeeze his hand briefly. Not with pity, he thought, but with fellow feeling—and that gave him the confidence to open up to her.

'Apparently she and dad were going through a rocky patch. He had a two-month secondment up in Edinburgh and my mum had an affair with an actor who came into the coffee shop where she worked while my dad—well, the man I grew up thinking was my dad—was away. I'm the result.'

He shook his head to clear it. 'I always thought my parents had the perfect marriage, something real. They've been together for thirty-seven years. I thought they were happy.' How wrong he'd been.

'I guess you never know what's really going on in someone else's marriage,' Dani said.

And it had made him wonder how happy his parents were now. Had his mother had other affairs to stop her being bored and lonely while his father worked long hours? Had his father looked elsewhere, too?

The news had totally shaken his belief in love and marriage. Especially when Lara had then started to back off from him. He'd thought she loved him. Obviously not as much as he'd believed, because it had been so easy for her to walk away.

'Did the other man know about you?' Dani asked.

He nodded. 'Mum told him when she realised she was pregnant. He said he had the chance of starring in a TV series in America and having a kid would hold him back. So he dumped my mum and went to Hollywood. Then Dad came back from Edinburgh, and she made things up with him. She told him a couple of weeks later that she was pregnant, and I guess she must've fudged her dates because I always believed I was a couple of weeks early.'

'There's no chance she might've been wrong about her dates and you could be your dad's child?' she asked.

He shook his head. 'I always wondered why I never looked anything like him. Now I know—it's because we don't actually share any genes.'

'Why did your mum tell you about it now?'

'More than thirty years later?' He grimaced. 'Because Stephen—the actor she had an affair with—contacted her. It took him a while to find her. We'd moved a couple of times, and he didn't know if she'd stayed with my dad or not, or if she'd changed her name.'

She waited, and finally he let the words that had been choking him spill out.

'Stephen was diagnosed with Huntington's and his doctor told him he needed to tell his children.'

'Did he have any other children?' she asked.

He shook his head. 'Just me. And, before you ask, no. I haven't taken a test to find out if I have the faulty gene.'

'I wasn't going to ask,' she said mildly. 'It's none of my business.'

He sighed. 'Sorry. Mum keeps nagging me. I'm over-touchy about it.'

'I think anyone would be, in your shoes. There's a fifty-fifty chance you've inherited Huntington's. Taking the test could set your mind at rest—or it could blow your world apart completely. It takes time to get your head round that and decide whether you really want to know.'

She actually understood?

He wasn't just being stubborn and unreasonable and difficult about things?

'Have you talked to your dad about it?' she asked.

'Which one?'

'Either. Both.'

But he knew which one she meant. 'The one I grew up with. No. It's been a bit strained between all of us ever since Mum told him. He moved out for a few weeks afterwards. They're back together again now, but it's very fragile. I think seeing me kind of rubs his nose in it—I'm a physical reminder of the fact that Mum had an affair. So I'm keeping my distance and letting them patch things up without me getting in the way and making things worse.'

'Were you close growing up?' she asked.

'Yes.' That was the bit that hurt most. Because of this mess, Alex had lost his real dad, the man he'd looked up to right from childhood. Why couldn't Stephen have just continued being selfish and kept the news to himself, instead of making the effort to find his son? How ironic that maybe Stephen had tried to be unselfish for once in his life but instead had performed the ultimate selfish act and broken up a family. 'I idolised my dad. One of the reasons I became a doctor is because I wanted to follow in his footsteps—it's a different specialty, because he was an orthopod and I fell in love with obstetrics during my placement year, but I always looked up to him and he always had time for me.' And now all that was ruined. It was very clear to Alex that Will Morgan didn't see him as his son any more.

'Maybe you need to talk to him on your own, without your mum,' Dani suggested. 'The news must've been a huge shock to him. And maybe he's not looking at you as a reminder of her affair, Alex. Maybe he's worried that you're going to reject him as some kind of interloper, and now you know he isn't your biological dad maybe you don't think of him as your dad any more, so he's try-ing to take a step back and not put any pressure on you.'

It was the first time Alex had considered that. He'd been so sure that his father had seen him as a horrible reminder of his wife's affair. But was the real reason that Will had backed away that he was scared Alex was going to reject him?

'Thank you,' he said. Truly grateful to her for making him see things differently, he reached over and squeezed her hand.

Mistake.

Because touching her again, this time not accidentally, made his skin tingle.

And this really wasn't the most appropriate time for his libido to wake up.

Clearly his touch didn't have quite the same effect on Dani, because, totally businesslike, she asked, 'Have you met your biological father?'

'Yes. I went over to America a week or so after Mum told me about him. It wasn't the easiest of meetings and Stephen didn't really acknowledge me—though he wasn't that well. I did go to see him again a few days later and we managed to talk a bit.' He shrugged. 'I didn't feel any real connection to him.' Nothing like the connection he'd once had with Will Morgan, the man he'd grown up believing was his father. 'Stephen's my biological father, but it doesn't feel as if that means anything at all.'

'It takes more than sperm to make someone a dad. We see that every day at work,' she said.

He liked how clear-sighted she was. 'But meeting him, seeing how much his health had deteriorated, made me think,' he said. 'Stephen's partner Catriona had become his carer, and I didn't want to put that kind of potential burden on my partner. So when I came back from America I ended my engagement.'

She raised an eyebrow. 'Did you give her the choice, or did you make the decision for her?'

The question caught him on the raw—she'd said she wasn't judging him, but the tone of her voice said otherwise. That he was at fault for setting Lara free. 'It was more a case of jumping before I was pushed.'

'I'm sorry. Just the way you said it...'

He sighed. 'Yes, I ended it. But she'd backed away from me ever since I told her about the Huntington's. I don't blame her. Would you want to get married to someone, knowing that in twenty years' time or even less you'll have to be their carer?'

'Maybe. Maybe not. Though that's what marriage is meant to be—in sickness and in health. Whether you know about it beforehand or not.' She looked him straight in the eye. 'But I'd want the choice to be mine, not made for me.'

'I saw the relief in her eyes,' he said softly. 'Because if she'd been the one to end it, people would've thought she was heartless.'

'Wasn't she?'

'Not everyone can cope with that kind of burden. Stephen was lucky, because Catriona really loved him and was prepared to look after him. But it's a massive task—one I wouldn't want to dump on someone.' He blew out a breath. 'Lara wasn't heartless. She just couldn't cope. And I didn't want her to stay with me out of duty or feel bad for ending it.'

'So you ended it. Making you look like the heartless one.'

'Or the one whose life went into meltdown.' He sighed. 'I pushed everyone else away after that, too. My best friend. Friends at work. I didn't want to be a burden to anyone. And the very last thing I wanted was pity.'

'Noted,' she said. 'Do you miss her?'

'I did at first, but not any more.' Not since he'd stopped believing in love. 'Everything's different now. I took a sabbatical to try and get my head round the situation. I went travelling.'

'Did it help?' she asked.

'Not that much,' he admitted. 'I really missed work. At least there I know who I am. I thought maybe a new start in a new place would help, and that's why I accepted the job at Muswell Hill.'

And that explained a lot, Dani thought. She understood now why Alex kept people at a distance, not even making friendships at work: because he knew he had a fifty per cent chance of inheriting Huntington's and didn't want to be a potential burden to anyone. But at the same time he was missing out on so much. It would be years and years before he started showing symptoms, if he had them at all. Years and years of being isolated and alone. What kind of life was that?

'I know you don't want pity and I'm not dispensing that—but this new start isn't helping, is it?' she asked softly.

'The job is. I love what I do.' He sighed. 'But the rest of it's still going round my head. Especially now.'

'Now?' she prompted softly.

'My mother left me a message on my answering machine last night. Stephen died the night before last.'

So any chance Alex might've had for closure with his father was gone for good. 'How old was he?'

'Fifty-seven. Twenty-two years older than I am right now. And, from what his partner told me, the last five years of his life were barely worth living. In the end he couldn't do anything for himself—he couldn't wash himself, he couldn't feed himself, he couldn't get out of a chair or walk without help. He needed total nursing care.' He dragged in a breath. 'That's not living, Dani, it's just *existence*.'

She reached over to squeeze his hand again. 'It's a tough thing to face. But it's not necessarily going to happen to you, Alex. Yes, there's a fifty per cent chance you've inherited Huntington's, but there's also a fifty per cent chance you haven't.'

'And the only way to know for sure is to take the test.' He looked at her, unsmiling. 'Which I don't want to do.'

She didn't think he was a coward. He had been brave enough to end his engagement and take the blame when he hadn't been the one at fault. If he tested positive, she was pretty sure he'd be able to face up to the implications. 'What's stopping you?' she asked, keeping her voice kind.

'There doesn't seem to be any point. If I'm positive, there's nothing anyone can do about it. I can't make any lifestyle changes or take any kind of treatment that would prevent me developing Huntington's or even stave it off for a while. And if the test is positive, it'd crucify my mother—she'd blame herself, even though she couldn't possibly have known that Stephen had Huntington's when they conceived me.' He sighed. 'And I think that the guilt, the sheer pressure on her, would finally crack my parents' marriage. I need to give them the chance to rebuild their relationship.'

'Or maybe not knowing one way or the other is like having a sentence hanging over them and putting just as much pressure on them,' she said. 'What if the test is negative?'

'I don't know. If I'm honest about it,' he said, his expression grim, 'I think my parents would still be struggling. For all I know, they've been unhappy for years.'

'You can't be responsible for someone else's relationship,' she said gently.

'I just feel so guilty,' he said. 'My father's dead—and I don't feel anything.'

'I'd be more surprised,' she said, 'if you were utterly devastated by the death of someone you'd only met twice, who'd spent most of your life denying that you had anything to do with him, and who from the sound of it treated your mother quite badly.'

He looked at her. 'You really tell it like it is, don't you?'

She shrugged. 'It's who I am. Bossy.'

'No, you're honest. And you've put things into perspective for me. Thank you.'

'You're welcome.' She squeezed his hand again. 'And I want to remind you that what you've told me tonight will stay completely confidential.'

'I appreciate that. You're nice,' he said. 'Kind.'

'Hmm. I've been told I'm too opinionated and I think I'm always right.'

He couldn't help smiling. 'Probably by someone who couldn't organise their way out of a paper bag or make a decision.'

'Oh, he made a decision, all right.' The words came out before she could stop them.

'Your ex?' he guessed.

'It's not a pretty story. I'll give you the short version.' And the short version didn't sting as much because she kept the emotion out of it. 'He had an affair, I had absolutely no idea, she fell pregnant—and he left me for her on Christmas Eve last year.'

He winced. 'That's horrible timing.'

Yeah. She knew. And it was unbelievable how many songs were about being abandoned at Christmas. She'd stopped listening to music on the radio or streamed through her phone, because the songs just made her feel worse.

And what a Christmas gift. Hello, darling, I want a divorce.

Only a few months before that, she'd suggested trying for a baby. Leo had shut her down, and she'd tried to stem the longing. It had hurt so much to find out he was having the baby he'd refused her with someone else, and to realise that after all it wasn't the baby he hadn't wanted—it was her.

Because he hadn't loved her any more.

Because she wasn't loveable.

'Though I guess he did the right thing, standing by the mother of his child.' She spread her hands. 'Someone always gets hurt in that kind of situation. It just happened to be me, this time round.'

'For what it's worth,' Alex said, 'I think your ex was utterly stupid. Why have an affair when you're already married to a woman who's bright, full of energy and totally lovely?'

She smiled. 'There are answers to that, but they're a little cynical. And thank you for the compliment. I wasn't fishing.'

'I know. I was just stating a fact.'

'Thank you.' She paused. 'I thought you didn't like me. Because of the way you are at work.'

He shook his head. 'It's not that. I didn't want to make friends with anyone.'

'Don't punish yourself,' she said gently. 'None of this Huntington's thing is your fault. And it doesn't mean you can't have friends.'

'I don't want to end up being a burden to anyone.'

'Firstly,' she said, 'you don't know for sure that you have it. Secondly, if you do have it, medicine might have advanced enough for there to be some sort of treatment by the time you start getting symptoms. Thirdly, Huntington's is really rare, but there are a lot of other medical conditions where people need a lot of support in the end stages. It's miserable enough suffering from a difficult medical condition, without cutting yourself off from people and making yourself lonely as well.' She paused.

'My grandfather had dementia. He didn't want to be a burden, so while he was still in the early stages he made my mum promise to put him in residential care rather than run herself ragged trying to care for him and look after me and do her job. She felt horribly guilty about it, but finding him a care home meant she could spend time with him as his daughter rather than his carer and that made things a lot easier for both of them. Yes, it was still hard for her, losing a little bit more of him every time she saw him, but he didn't feel he was a burden. And she's made me promise that if she gets dementia I'll do the same for her. There are ways round things.'

'Sometimes it's hard to see them.'

'Sometimes you're too close to things and it takes someone else to see it for you,' she pointed out.

'True.' He paused. 'I'd better let you get on. Thank you for the pizza and the pep talk.'

'Any time.' She stood up. 'Hey. Before you go.'

He turned to her, expecting her to say something; instead, to his shock, she put her arms round him, holding him close for a few moments.

When was the last time anyone had hugged him? The last time he'd actually let anyone hug him?

Months ago. What felt like a lifetime ago.

'What was that for?' he asked.

'Because,' she said softly, 'it seems to me you've had a rough few months, you've been a little bit too noble and self-sacrificing, and in the circumstances I think you've been needing someone to hold you for way too long.'

She was right. Except now it made him feel like a man who'd trudged through the desert for days and had finally found an oasis. Unable to stop himself, he put his arms round her and held her close, breathing in the soft vanilla scent of her shampoo.

And from holding her it was only one step to sliding his cheek against hers. Turning towards her. Letting his lips touch the corner of her mouth. And then finally kissing her properly, losing himself in the sweetness of her mouth.

It suddenly slammed into him what he was doing.

Kissing Danielle Owens.

He had no right to do this.

He pulled back and looked at her in anguish. 'I'm sorry. I shouldn't have done that.'

'No?' She traced his lower lip with her fingertip, and it made him ache.

'This is a bad idea,' he said. 'I'm not in a place where I could even consider asking you out, and offering you a fling would be—well, not very honourable.'

'When my divorce came through,' she said, 'I made a pact with Hayley, my best friend. We agreed that this is the Year of Saying Yes.'

'The Year of Saying Yes?' He didn't quite understand.

'It means you say yes to every opportunity that makes your life happier, even if it's only for a little while. I was supposed to be going to Iceland with Hayley—but I broke my foot so I couldn't go. Though I made her agree to go on her own, so she got to see all the things on her bucket list: the midnight sun, watching whales in the sea, walking on a glacier. I'm hideously jealous, because a lot of them were on my list, too—but no way was I going to hold her back. And she admitted I was right to make her go because she had a wonderful time.'

'So what are you saying?'

'I'm saying,' she said, 'that maybe you could do the same. It doesn't have to be a year of saying yes. Six months, maybe, or even a week.' She paused. 'Or just tonight.'

His breath caught. 'Are you suggesting…?'

'I'm saying that you need to stop thinking and start doing. Live in the moment. No strings.'

Make love with Dani. Right at that moment, he wanted

it more than he could ever remember wanting anything. But he had to be sensible and hold himself back. 'There's just one tiny, tiny thing. Given that I might be carrying a faulty chromosome,' he said, 'I don't want to take any risks of passing it on. And I don't have a condom.'

'Whereas I do,' she said. 'Which isn't to say that the Year of Saying Yes means I sleep with every man I meet.'

He didn't think that Dani was the type to sleep around. Far from it. 'Have you actually slept with anyone since Christmas Eve?' he asked.

'No, and if I'm honest I didn't sleep with Leo very much in the last six months of our marriage,' she admitted. 'But I'm prepared now, in case I do meet someone.'

Someone.

Him.

The possibilities made every nerve-ending tingle.

'So have you slept with anyone since you ended your engagement?' she asked.

'No,' he admitted.

'Which means this is going to be faintly awkward and embarrassing, and there's no guarantee that either of us will remember what we're supposed to do.'

He couldn't help smiling. Which meant he'd smiled twice in one evening. *Twice in eight months.* And it was all thanks to Dani. 'That's really terrible, considering what we both do for a living.'

'Maybe we should just stop overthinking it,' she said.

'The Year of Saying Yes?'

'Or six months. Or a week. Or just tonight,' she said. 'Maybe we should just consider this a rebound thing. No consequences, no worries, just a moment out of time for both of us.'

She was right. They were both overthinking it. And

it sounded as if her world had been shattered, too, by her ex. Maybe tonight they could salvage something for both of them.

He kissed her. 'Yes.'

CHAPTER THREE

IT WAS THE first time Dani could ever remember propositioning anyone. And in some ways she was taking advantage of Alex; he'd opened his heart to her and told her exactly why he was keeping a distance between himself and the rest of the human race. He was vulnerable. Hurting.

Then again, so was she. She'd spent months trying to convince herself that she was over Leo. She didn't love her ex any more; but she was finding it hard to get past the knowledge that she hadn't been enough for him. That something in her was lacking. That maybe she was too bossy and unloveable—and that was why he hadn't wanted to have a baby with her.

She hadn't even told her best friend about that bit, feeling too ashamed of herself. Other people had it much worse—Hayley had had to bury the love of her life when she was only thirty years old—and Dani knew she was just being a whiny, selfish brat about her own situation.

But just maybe she and Alex could help each other feel better. If only for a little while.

She stroked his face. 'I'm glad it's a yes.'

He turned his head to press a kiss into her palm. 'Me, too.'

His blue-green eyes had darkened. Gratifyingly so. And Dani felt desire kick deep inside her.

'Then let's go somewhere more comfortable.'

She'd half expected him to hold her hand, but she wasn't prepared for him to scoop her up in his arms—as if he wanted her so much that he couldn't wait. It shocked her and thrilled her at the same time.

'Which door?' he asked when he carried her into the hallway.

'On your right,' she said.

He finessed the door handle, switched on the overhead light and closed the curtains, all without dropping her.

And then he let her slide down his body so she was left in no doubt about how much he wanted her.

She reached up to him and kissed him.

He untucked her shirt from her skirt, and unbuttoned it really, really slowly, keeping his gaze fixed on hers the whole time. Whenever his fingers brushed against her, it made her skin tingle.

'My turn,' she said, and undid his shirt. She blew out a breath. 'Nice musculature, Dr Morgan.'

He inclined his head to acknowledge the compliment. 'Thank you.'

She pushed the soft cotton off his shoulders. 'Nice arms.'

In return, he pushed her shirt off her shoulders. 'Turn round.'

Not sure where he was going with this, she did so.

'Nice back, Dr Owens.' And then he kissed the nape of her neck before loosening her hair from the scrunchie she kept it in at work.

Her knees went weak. Alex's touch was doing things to her that she'd forgotten could even happen.

'May I?' he asked, his fingers at the clasp of her bra.

'It's the Year of Saying Yes,' she reminded him, though she liked the fact that he'd asked.

'I know. But if you change your mind about this...'

'I'm not going to change my mind,' she said.

He unsnapped her bra and let the lacy garment fall to the floor, then slid his arms round her and cupped her breasts. 'Beautiful,' he said, and kissed his way along her shoulder.

Desire shivered through her. 'Alex.'

'I know. Me, too.' He turned her to face him and kissed her lightly. 'You're gorgeous.'

She hadn't felt it. Not for months and months and months. She'd felt ugly and rejected and unloveable, and hated herself even more for being so self-indulgent when so many worse things were happening in the world. But Alex's touch was helping to salve the bruise that went right through her.

'So are you,' she said.

She paused with her fingers on the waistband of his trousers. 'May I?'

'Yes,' he whispered, and the huskiness of his voice sent a thrill down her spine.

She undid the button, lowered the zip and eased the material over his hips. The trousers pooled at his feet and he stepped out of them. She picked them up and hung them neatly over the back of her chair, and Alex laughed softly.

'What?'

'Very organised.'

'If you'd been wearing jeans, I would've left them on the floor. But these are your work—'

He stopped her by kissing her. 'I was teasing. Actually,

I really like the way you just sort everything out without comment or fuss. It's adorable.'

That hadn't been what Leo had said. Her ex had seen her as a control freak. An emasculating bitch. And Dani wasn't entirely sure that her best friend was right when Hayley had said it was simply Leo trying to make excuses for his behaviour and pin the blame on her.

'Dani,' Alex said, his voice gentle. 'The deal was we're not thinking. We're just feeling. Tonight is tonight.'

'Yeah. Sorry.'

He drew her into his arms and stroked her hair. 'Your ex was incredibly selfish and incredibly stupid. Don't blame yourself.'

Much, much easier said than done.

'No,' she fibbed.

'Dani.' He tilted her chin upwards, making her meet his eyes. 'You're lovely. Don't let anyone make you think otherwise.'

His kindness almost brought tears to her eyes.

He slid his hands down her sides. 'Right now, you're wearing too much. And I'm not happy about your standing around in that walking cast.' He groaned. 'And that makes me feel horrible. I'm pushing myself onto an injured woman.'

She wasn't sure how much was theatrical teasing and how much he meant it, but the teasing note in his voice made her feel better. 'It's removable. And if you carry me to bed it'll take the pressure off my foot.' Pressure that wasn't really there in the first place, but she was going along with his line of whimsy.

He slid the zip of her skirt downwards, got her to step out of it, and then folded it neatly and hung it on the chair with his trousers. 'I'm a neat freak, too,' he said.

Dani was grateful for that.

'And you're beautiful, but this overhead light is a little too harsh.'

'I'll switch the bedside light on if you deal with the main light,' she said.

'Deal.'

And funny how the softer light made the room feel so much more intimate.

She'd never shared this bed with anyone, and part of her felt apprehensive about sharing it now. Was she doing the right thing? Was she just setting herself up for heartbreak?

But then she stopped thinking as Alex dropped to his knees in front of her and peeled her tights downwards. He nuzzled her abdomen, and she couldn't help the sharp intake of breath.

He undid her cast and removed it gently, then finished taking off her tights, letting her lean on him for support. 'You mentioned something about carrying you to bed.'

'Uh-huh.' She stole a kiss. 'Strictly speaking, I should've been wearing a Regency dress and you should be in a frock coat and a flowing shirt with a waistcoat, cravat and silk breeches.'

He raised an eyebrow. 'Just call me Darcy, hmm?'

'Something like that.'

'It's too late for the outfit,' he said. 'But I can still do the carrying. Though, before I forget myself completely, where do you keep your condoms?'

'Top drawer of my bedside cabinet,' she said.

'Would you mind if I...?'

'Sure,' she said. Whatever she'd previously thought about Alex being rude and difficult, she'd changed her mind. He had perfect manners.

And then she stopped thinking as he scooped her up and carried her over to her bed. He pulled the duvet back and laid her back against the pillows. And she felt weirdly shy all of a sudden; he must've sensed it, because he climbed into bed next to her, pulled the duvet over both of them and drew her into his arms.

'You can still change your mind,' he said. 'The Year of Saying Yes is about seizing opportunities, not making yourself do something you don't want to do.'

'I want to do this,' she said. 'But it's been a while.'

'Same here. And we agreed, no pressure. This is just for tonight. A moment out of time.'

'Never to be spoken of again.'

'Exactly. And now we stop speaking,' he said, and kissed her.

And after that it was easy to stop thinking, stop speaking, and just lose herself in pleasure—to let herself enjoy touching him, exploring the hardness of his muscles and the softness of his skin.

Alex dipped his head and nuzzled the hollows of Dani's collar bones. He loved the way her skin felt against his mouth, and the soft fruity scent of her shower gel. She arched back against the bed and he moved lower, taking one nipple into his mouth and sucking hard. She slid her hands into his hair, urging him on.

And he forgot all the nightmares that had plagued him over the last few months. All he could think of was Dani, and how much he wanted to be inside her. How much he wanted to give as much pleasure as he took.

He kissed his way down over her abdomen, then shifted to kneel between her legs.

'Alex, yes,' she whispered as his tongue stroked along her sex.

He teased her, flicking the tip of her clitoris with the tip of his tongue, until her hands clenched in his hair and her body tightened beneath his mouth. And then he ripped open the foil packet he'd taken from her bedside cabinet, slid the condom over his erection and pushed into her.

'Alex,' she whispered, and he held still, letting her body adjust to the feel of him inside her.

Her dark eyes were wide with pleasure, and he loved the knowledge that he'd been able to do that for her.

'I wanted the first time to be for you,' he said softly.

Her eyes filled with tears, as if she wasn't used to her feelings being considered like that. Then again, given the little she'd told him about her past, consideration hadn't been high on her ex's agenda.

'Hey. It's the Year of Saying Yes,' he said.

She smiled. 'Yes.'

And then she took it to another level, wrapping her legs round him to draw him deeper and tensing her muscles round him.

'Oh. Yes.' The breath hissed out of him.

And then he stopped thinking, instead responding to the physicality between them and revelling in the way she made him feel.

By the time he climaxed, his head was spinning; and then he felt her body rippling round his as her own climax hit. He wrapped his arms round her and held her tightly until it had all ebbed away.

'I'd better deal with the condom,' he said finally.

'There are fresh towels in the bathroom. Help yourself to anything you need.' She paused. 'Stay tonight.'

He ought to say no. Put distance between them. Go back to being sensible and isolated.

But every bit of him yearned to say yes. To spend the night with her wrapped in his arms, to let her take the loneliness away—and to make her feel less alone, too.

As if his dilemma showed on his face, she said softly, 'It's the Year of Saying Yes.'

So what else could he do?

'Yes.'

The next morning, Alex woke, feeling slightly disorientated: this wasn't his bed, and he was spooned against a warm female body, with his arm wrapped round her waist.

Dani.

Thanks to her, his heart felt lighter than it had for months. But it still didn't change the stark reality of his situation. Even though he wished things could be different, last night had to be just that: last night. A one-off. Something that had healed some of the pain for both of them, but still a temporary solution.

He was about to try and disentangle himself from her when there was a sharp shrill, a groan, and then she reached out to hit the top of the alarm clock and the noise stopped.

And then she turned to face him. 'Good morning.'

'Good morning,' he said warily.

She pressed her palm briefly against his cheek. 'Don't look so worried. I usually hit the gym before work, so you've got plenty of time to have breakfast and then get back to your own place for clean clothes.'

Of course. Dani was organisation personified. 'Thank you,' he said.

'There are clean towels in the airing cabinet, if you'd like the first shower. And there's a new spare toothbrush on the middle shelf of the bathroom cabinet.'

She thought of everything.

'I'll go and make some coffee and sort out some breakfast.'

He frowned. 'Isn't that going to make you late for the gym?'

'No. I'm going to skip it today,' she said. 'And before you start feeling guilty about it, it's nothing to do with you and everything to do with pacing myself with my foot.'

'Thank you.' He paused. 'Dani, we need to talk about this. If things were different...' He grimaced and shook his head. 'But they're not. I'm sorry. I feel bad about this, but I can't even consider having a relationship. Not with the Huntington's thing hanging over me.'

'I know. And it's the same for me. I'm not looking for a relationship right now either. We agreed last night that it was just going to be last night. Between you and me. Never to be spoken of again.'

The problem was, he wanted to repeat it. Waking up with her in his arms had felt so good. But he couldn't be selfish enough to ask her. 'Uh-huh.'

'Which means we can be professional with each other at work,' she said.

'Agreed.' He paused. 'Though we still need to sort out the departmental Christmas meal.'

'Maybe we can have a second try at it tomorrow evening,' she said. 'Maybe, strictly as colleagues, we can try the different meal options between us—actually, there are four, so either we can drag some colleagues along or we can do it on two evenings. Or just one evening and be super-greedy.'

Strictly as colleagues: so this wasn't a date masquerading under another name. 'Do you have anyone in mind?'

'We could...' She paused and shook her head. 'Actually, no. We'll keep it to just us.'

'All right.' And funny how the guilt he'd felt had just drained away.

'Go have your shower,' she said, and climbed out of the bed.

Alex's pulse spiked. Just as he'd thought, the first time he'd met her, she was a pocket Venus, all curves—but her curves were toned from a mixture of running and her programme in the gym. She was utterly gorgeous.

And his thoughts were completely inappropriate. They were supposed to be just colleagues from now on.

He closed his eyes, and then he heard her laugh. 'It's a bit late to be shy, Alex.'

'I guess.' And when he opened his eyes again he saw that she was wearing a fluffy towelling bath robe.

'Sorry, I don't have a spare bath robe to offer to lend you—and if I did, it wouldn't fit you anyway. But I'll leave you to sort yourself out while I sort out breakfast.'

'Thanks.'

When he'd showered and dressed, he joined her in the kitchen.

She was drinking coffee and finishing a piece of wholemeal toast spread generously with peanut butter. 'What would you like?' she asked. 'Toast, oatmeal, yoghurt?'

'Toast would be lovely—but I'll make it,' he said. 'You're not wearing your walking cast, so you're absolutely not waiting on me.'

'Anyone would think you were in cahoots with my best friend,' she said, rolling her eyes. 'She nags me about my cast, too. And I hate the thing.'

'The more you wear it, the more quickly you'll heal and can get rid of it.'

'The word "rest" wasn't in my vocabulary until August this year, and I hate feeling so constrained,' she said, rolling her eyes. 'OK. Help yourself to breakfast. Milk's in the fridge and coffee's in the pot. I'll go and get showered and dressed.'

Funny how easy she was to be with, Alex thought. And he was in a much better place than he'd been in last night. Enough to let him be nosy and look at the photographs held on her fridge with magnets while he ate his toast.

He recognised the woman with her in several of the photographs—Hayley from the emergency department—and guessed that this was Dani's best friend. There were others from what he assumed were team nights out; there was one where she was holding a biscuit tin above her head as if it were a trophy, and there were half a dozen midwives with her.

'That,' Dani said, coming to stand beside him and peering at the photograph, 'is the only time in the last year that we've beaten the emergency department in the monthly pub quiz. How's your general knowledge?'

'I...' Oh, help. He didn't like where this was going.

'I'm guessing it's good,' she said. 'The Emergency lot are getting very cheeky about their winning streak. We need a secret weapon to take them down a peg or two. I think you'd fit the bill rather nicely.'

'I'm not sure I can handle a crowd,' he said.

'Then you can work up to it,' she said. 'Maybe start

by having lunch with a couple of us from the ward today, instead of a sandwich on your own and hiding behind a journal.'

'Maybe.' Though he had a feeling he wasn't going to have a choice in the matter. Dani was clearly in fixer mode.

She glanced at her watch. 'And I guess you need to get going.'

'I'll do the washing up first.'

'If you do, you'll be late,' she said with a smile. 'And there's not that much to do. Go. I'll see you at work.'

'OK. And thank you.'

'Pleasure.' She rested her hand briefly on his forearm, and it was all he could do to stop himself lifting her hand to his mouth and pressing a kiss into her palm. 'Alex, I meant what I said. Nothing you told me last night will go any further than me, but any time you need a friend to talk something over, you know where I am.'

A friend.

If only she could've been more than that.

'I appreciate it.'

'And remember, the only person who decides when to do that test is you. Which is when you're ready, and not a second before then.'

How good it felt to have her batting his corner. To have someone who understood and wasn't judging him.

'I'll see you at work,' she said. 'And I'll book us a table for tomorrow night so we can agree the menu.'

'Sounds good,' he said.

Dani texted him later to say their table was booked for seven, tomorrow evening. And, just as he'd suspected, that day she made him join her and Jas, one of the midwives, for lunch. Although he'd been antsy at the idea, given that he'd kept himself at such a distance from everyone in the previous two months, he was surprised to find himself relaxing with them.

Though at the same time he was so aware of Dani. How she'd felt in his arms. The warmth of her skin against his. He shook himself. Now was really not an appropriate time to remember that.

'I'm glad I'm getting to know you a bit better,' Jas said. 'You're good with our mums, but I was beginning to worry that you were one of those consultants who prefers to keep a distance between himself and the midwives.'

He knew the type she meant, and it was an attitude he hated. 'I'm not. And I'm sorry I've come across as a snob with a superiority complex.'

'When really you're just a little bit shy,' Dani said.

'And sweet,' Jas added.

He couldn't help laughing. 'I wouldn't describe myself as sweet either.'

'You'll do,' Jas said with a grin.

Alex had missed this kind of teasing camaraderie. Even though part of him felt that he needed to keep his distance so he wouldn't become a burden to anyone, maybe Dani had a point about the potential of a horrible disease being enough to deal with without isolating himself into the bargain.

He didn't get to see anything of Dani the next day, between Theatre and two busy clinics. But she'd left him a text reminding him to eat sparsely because they were having three courses and they might have to double up on the pudding.

They'd arranged to meet at the pub; he'd just bought a drink and was leaning against the bar when she walked in, wearing smart trousers to hide her walking cast teamed with a pretty top. He realised that she was wearing lipstick—something she didn't do at work. So was she wearing it for his benefit? His pulse rate spiked and he really had to resist the urge to kiss it off her.

He raised his hand to get her attention; she smiled and walked over to him.

And funny how her smile made his heart felt as if it had done a somersault.

Colleagues and friends *only*, he reminded himself. It wasn't fair to either of them to act on this attraction. 'Can I get you a drink?' he asked.

'Thanks. Sparkling water, please.'

Once they'd got their drinks, they made their way to the restaurant. After the waiter had shown them to their table and brought menus, Dani took out a file with the details of the Christmas meal.

'OK. Because our departmental Christmas meal is on a weeknight, we can get away with organising it this late,' she said. 'There are a couple of other places that can fit us in, but I've eaten here with Hayley a few times so I know the food's good. We get the function room to ourselves, and once we've eaten they're going to move the tables so we've got a dance floor. Maybe Baby are doing the music.'

'Maybe Baby?' Alex asked, mystified.

'They're kind of our house band,' Dani explained. 'Half of the band's from our department and half's from Paediatrics. From our department, Anton plays lead guitar and Gilly plays the bass, then from Paediatrics, Keely's the singer and Marty's the drummer. They play at most of the hospital functions and they're really good—

they play everything from the latest chart stuff through to oldies.'

'Sounds good. So really we need to focus on the menu, crackers...maybe a Secret Santa?'

'Jas is organising the Secret Santa—she's doing the names next week,' Dani said. 'But yes, we need to agree on the menu and crackers. There's an option to donate money to cancer research instead of having novelties in the crackers.'

'We should do that,' he said. 'Novelties always get left on the table; all we really need are the paper hats and terrible jokes.'

'Agreed. So. Food. They sent me a list of options, and I checked the normal evening menu on the website and some of our options are available tonight,' she said. 'Carrot and coriander soup—well, soup's a soup. Then there's the salmon mousse with pickled cucumber and rye bread, which covers fish; ham hock terrine with apple chutney, which covers meat; and what do you think about arancini with a Parmesan crisp for the veggie option?'

'Sounds good,' he said. 'What about the main course? I'm assuming there's the traditional turkey with all the trimmings.'

'There is,' she said. 'And roast sirloin, so that gives us two traditional options.'

'So we need a veggie option and a fish option.' Funny, he'd thought this was going to be dull. But it was actually fun. Or maybe it was just because it meant he could spend time with Dani.

He was really going to have to be careful.

'There's a leek, chestnut and cranberry tart that sounds nice,' she said. 'Or a butternut squash risotto.'

'Chestnuts are maybe more Christmassy,' he said. 'What about the fish?'

'Sea bass or salmon.'

'We've got salmon in the first course,' he said. 'So maybe sea bass would be better.'

'Perfect. And then for pudding there's traditional Christmas pudding with brandy sauce; passionfruit cheesecake; dark chocolate torte; and cheese and crackers.'

'Coffee after?' he checked.

She nodded. 'With Christmas petit fours.'

'Perfect. OK. So what are we trying?'

'This is why I told you to eat sparsely,' she said. 'I can already vouch for the Sunday roast dinner here, so maybe if we order the fish and the tart. And Christmas pudding and cheese and crackers are standard everywhere, so we can get away with ordering the cheesecake and the chocolate. But that leaves us four starters.'

'Bring it on,' he said with a grin.

Alex Morgan, now he'd thawed out a bit, was *nice*, Dani thought. More than nice. She really liked him.

It would be all too easy to lose her heart to him.

But his situation meant that he wasn't in the market for a relationship; and Dani had promised herself that never again would she fall for someone who couldn't love her all the way back. Leo's double betrayal had hurt her deeply. And although she'd agreed the Year of Saying Yes with Hayley, she'd done it purely to help her best friend move on from the tragedy of Evan's death. She wasn't sure she was ready to risk her own heart again. Leo had made her feel unloveable, and she wasn't going to put herself in another situation where she'd fallen for someone who didn't feel the same way.

She and Alex were strictly colleagues, she reminded herself. Friendship was as far as they could go. And that would have to be enough. Because the night they'd spent together couldn't be repeated.

CHAPTER FOUR

'DANIELLE OWENS SPEAKING,' Dani said, answering the phone.

'Dani? It's Hayley—we've got a patient coming in who's been in a car accident. She's thirty-two weeks. The paramedics have talked to me on the way in and it sounds as if we're looking at an abruption. She's in shock, she's in pain, her uterus is woody and they can't feel the foetal parts easily.'

An abruption—where the placenta was torn away from the uterus—was a life-threatening emergency and there was a strong chance that the baby could die.

'She'll be here in about ten minutes. Can you come down?' Hayley asked.

'I'm on my way,' Dani said. She put the phone down and grabbed the first midwife she could find. 'Gilly, I've just had a call from the emergency department. We've got a mum coming in at thirty-two weeks with a suspected abruption, so I need an anaesthetist and a theatre, please.'

'I'm on it,' Gilly said. 'And I'll get the neonatal special care unit on standby.'

'Thanks, Gilly.' Dani knocked on Alex's door and filled him in on the situation. 'Given that we might have to operate, can I grab you now?'

'Of course. I'm not due in clinic for another hour, but I'll make sure everyone knows where I am if I'm going to be late.' He closed the file he was working on and logged off the computer. 'What do you know about the mum?'

'The paramedics were called out to a car accident. She's in shock, has a woody uterus and it's hard to feel the baby.'

'That definitely sounds like a potential abruption,' he said. 'Let's keep our fingers crossed that the baby makes it as far as the hospital.'

They headed out of the ward, and her fingers brushed against his as they walked into the lift. How ridiculous that her skin should tingle when he touched her. He really needed to stop this. She was off limits. Colleagues only.

And oh, how he wished it could be otherwise.

Hayley met them at the emergency department.

'Do I need to introduce you to each other?' Dani asked.

'No, we've worked together a couple of times,' Alex said.

'That makes things easy, then,' Dani said. 'Haze, I've filled Alex in on the situation.'

'Good. I'll sort out blood tests and a cross-match of four units of blood, with fresh frozen plasma on standby as soon as she comes in, but in the meantime I have Hartmann's solution available,' Hayley said. 'The paramedics are giving her oxygen and putting an IV in. She's due here any minute now.'

'Thank you. We'll examine her and do an ultrasound,' Alex said. 'Do you have a portable machine here?'

'Yes. I'll make sure it's in Resus,' Hayley said.

'If the baby's still alive and mature enough to be delivered, we'll take her up to Theatre and do a section,' he said.

'And if the baby's not OK?' Dani asked.

'Then we know the mum will deliver the baby not that long afterwards, so we'll focus on the mum,' Alex said. 'We'll need to treat her for shock and try to avoid DIC.'

Disseminated intravascular coagulation was where the normal blood clotting process was disrupted. The blood formed small clots and couldn't flow properly through the tissues, leading to organ damage; at the same time, the patient could bleed heavily. And it was a life-threatening condition: between ten and fifty per cent of patients with DIC didn't make it.

He blew out a breath. 'Poor woman. I hope we can get her the right result.'

The paramedics came in and did the handover, and helped move Mrs Kirby from the trolley to the bed in Resus.

'Mrs Kirby, I'm Alex Morgan and I'm a consultant from the maternity department,' Alex said. 'This my colleague Dani from Maternity, and Hayley from the emergency department. I know you've been in a car accident and right now things seem very scary, but I'm going to examine you to see what's going on with the baby, if that's all right.'

'Is my baby OK?' Mrs Kirby took the oxygen mask off; her voice was high-pitched with panic. 'The paramedics couldn't feel the baby or get a heartbeat.'

It's sometimes difficult to feel what's happening because you're in a lot of pain and your uterus tends to feel hard in this sort of situation,' Dani explained. 'I know it's hard but try not to worry. Alex and I are going to do an ultrasound to see what's going on.'

'Can we call anyone for you?' Hayley asked.

'The paramedics already called my husband. He's on his way.'

'I'm going to examine you now,' Alex said. 'I'd like you to put the mask back on, and lift your hand or tap me if anything hurts.'

'I don't care about me,' Mrs Kirby said. 'I just want my baby to be OK.'

Dani held her hand and helped her put the oxygen mask back on. 'We'll do our best,' she said. When Alex examined Mrs Kirby, Dani could see from his expression that he wasn't happy: clearly her uterus felt woody.

'I can see there's no sign of a vaginal bleed,' he said. 'So I'm not going to do an internal examination.'

If blood from the detached placenta wasn't coming through the cervix, that meant the abruption was concealed—so it was more serious and they couldn't tell how much blood she'd lost.

'I need to take some blood from you so we can check it's clotting properly,' Hayley said, and quickly took the samples.

Dani had the portable ultrasound ready. 'I'm going to squeeze some gel onto your tummy now. It's exactly the same sort of scan you had for your dating scan and the twenty-week scan, so try not to worry,' she said gently.

She glanced over at Alex. He was holding Mrs Kirby's hand and looked white-faced and grim; clearly he didn't think this was going to be good news.

She swept the head of the scanner over Mrs Kirby's stomach. She couldn't see the abruption clearly, but on the screen she could just about see the baby moving. The heartbeat didn't look brilliant but, most importantly, it was *there.* She nodded at Alex.

'It's good news,' Alex said to Mrs Kirby. 'We can see the baby's heartbeat, so we're going to take you into Theatre for an emergency section and deliver the baby now.'

Mrs Kirby pulled off her mask again. 'Isn't thirty-two weeks too soon?

'The baby will be small and will need to be in Special Care for a while, but thirty-two weeks is still OK for delivery. The team here is really good,' Alex reassured her.

By time they went up to Theatre, the units of blood for transfusion were ready and the blood test results were back. To Dani's relief, the coagulation screen was reasonable and it looked as if they might be lucky and avoid a situation where their patient developed DIC. The transfusion was set up and, while Dani and Alex scrubbed up ready for the operation, the anaesthetist talked Mrs Kirby through the fact that was going to need a general anaesthetic for the birth, so her husband would have to wait outside rather than being there for the birth, but could see the baby straight away afterwards. Karin, the specialist from the neonatal special care team, was ready with the crib.

'Ready?' Alex asked.

Alex performed the section with Dani assisting; and although part of her admired how skilfully he worked, part of her was waiting desperately to hear that first cry. Had they done the section in time, or was it too late for the baby?

She only realised she'd been holding her breath when there was a thin wail. The sound she'd been waiting to hear.

'Well done, team,' Alex said.

'Not a brilliant first Apgar score, but he's starting to pink up now,' Karin said, sounding relieved.

'Nice work,' Dani said to Alex.

'Thanks.' He looked relieved. 'I'm just glad we were on time for the baby, though we're not out of the woods yet with the mum or the baby.' They hadn't had time to give her a steroid injection to help mature the baby's lungs, plus Dani knew that Mrs Kirby was more at risk of a post-partum haemorrhage because of the abruption.

'We'll keep a very close eye on her on the ward, and Special Care will have the baby under close monitoring,' she said.

'Do we have a camera here?' he asked. 'Or at least can someone take a photograph of the baby for Mrs Kirby before you take him off to Special Care? She's had a horrible experience and I don't want to make her wait until she's out of the recovery room before she sees him.'

'I'm on it,' Karin said.

Between them, Alex and Dani finished closing the incision and sewing all the layers together while Karin took a photograph and then the baby was taken off to the neonatal special care unit. And then finally the anaesthetist brought Mrs Kirby round.

'Wonderful news, Mrs Kirby. You've got a beautiful little boy,' Alex told her with a smile.

'Is he all right? Can I see him?'

'I'm afraid Karin's taken him to the neonatal special care unit, and we need to wait until you're fully round from the anaesthetic before we can take you to see him, but she did take a photograph for you first.' He handed her the photograph.

A tear trickled down her cheek. 'He's beautiful.'

'He's holding his own,' Alex told her. 'He's about three and a half pounds, which is a nice weight for a thirty-two-weeker.'

'He's got all his fingers and toes—including nails,' Dani said. 'Though you'll notice he's a bit wrinkly. He'll fill out and double his weight over the next two months.'

Mrs Kirby bit her lip. 'Is my husband here? Can he see the baby?'

'I think he might be in Special Care with your baby right now,' Dani said. 'I'll get hold of the team and ask him to come in to you.'

'Thank you,' Mrs Kirby said, the tears really flowing now. 'Thank you for saving my baby. You're both heroes.'

'We just did what we're trained to do,' Alex said, and squeezed her hand. 'We're going to take you to our recovery suite now, and then when we're happy you can go up to the ward. Once you're able to sit in a wheelchair, your husband will be able to take you to Special Care so you can see the baby.'

'It won't be too long,' Dani said, 'though I know any waiting's hard, especially in circumstances like yours. Try not to worry.'

'Just as long as the baby's all right.'

'He's in great hands,' Alex said.

Hands. Dani remembered just how good Alex was with his hands. How he'd made her feel. It would be oh, so easy to fall for him.

But that wasn't the agreement. And Alex had huge issues. He wasn't in a place where he could let himself fall for someone—and Dani didn't want to repeat her mistake of loving someone who didn't love her back.

They were strictly colleagues and friends, she reminded herself.

It was all they could be.

Alex dropped in to see the Kirbys at the end of his shift. 'How are you feeling?' he asked Mrs Kirby.

'I've had better days,' she said wryly. 'But I know I'm lucky to be here. And even luckier that our son's still alive.'

'Karin tells me he's a fighter and he's doing well,' Alex said.

'We'd like to name our baby Alex, after you,' Mrs Kirby said. 'If it wasn't for you, he wouldn't be here now.'

'It was teamwork, so it wasn't just me—it was the anaesthetist, Dani, Hayley and Karin as well,' Alex said.

But the words put a lump in his throat. A baby named after him. He wouldn't have a child of his own—a child who would maybe have had his name as a middle name, and maybe give that name to his own son. As an only child, Alex wouldn't be an uncle. There wouldn't be future generations to remember him with a smile. But his name, his work, would live on in this baby.

'Thank you. It's a real honour.'

She looked at him. 'Are you all right, Dr Morgan?'

'Yes.' He smiled at her. 'After all these years, I still get misty-eyed when I deliver a baby.' He checked her temperature and pulse, and wrote it up on her notes. 'I'll see you tomorrow,' he said. 'But if you need anything, just call one of the team. They're all really approachable on the ward.'

And it made him think on his way home. Life was short. And his own might turn out to be very messy indeed, so he couldn't waste time. He needed to repair the rift between himself and his family, and the sooner the better.

He took his phone from his pocket and texted his father to ask if he was free to meet up for a pint on Saturday evening—just the two of them. Maybe neutral territory would help them deal with the situation better. Though he really, really hoped that Dani was right about this—that Will feared he was going to be rejected, rather than being the one doing the rejecting.

He was beginning to think that either his text hadn't gone through or his father's phone was switched off when his phone beeped.

OK. Tell me where and when.

It was only then that Alex realised how tense he'd been, waiting and half expecting Will to refuse. In the end he named a pub roughly halfway between them that specialised in the kind of real ale he knew his father liked, and Will texted back a terse 'OK'. Then again, Alex knew better to read anything into the length of his father's reply. Will was a man of few words.

On Saturday evening, Will was already there at a table when Alex walked in, five minutes early.

'I've already bought you a pint,' he said. 'The Championship ale looked good on the board, and it's not bad.'

'Thanks.' Alex paused. 'So how are things?'

Will shrugged. 'Getting there, I suppose. Why did you want to see me without your mother?'

'I wanted to talk to you on your own about something.'

Will frowned. 'Are you in trouble?'

Yes, but not in the way his father was obviously fearing. Alex took a deep breath. 'I know we've always done all this English stiff upper lip business and never talked about our feelings, but I've been talking to a friend about the situation. She made me face up to a few things.'

'She?'

'We're just colleagues,' Alex said, before his father could make any more assumptions.

'Oh.' Will looked faintly disappointed.

'And I don't think I can make things any worse than they are right now,' Alex said, 'so I wanted to apologise.'

'Apologise?' Will looked surprised. 'For what?'

This felt as if he was ripping the top off his father's scars, but Alex knew it had to be done or the poison would continue to fester. 'For reminding you of Mum and Stephen every time you see me.'

Will looked shocked. 'Is that what you think?'

'Ever since Mum told us about what happened, you've pretty much avoided me, so that's what it feels like,' Alex said. 'But if it's not that seeing me brings up painful memories, then my friend might be right.'

'About what?'

Alex squirmed. This definitely ranked as one of the most uncomfortable conversations he'd ever had. But if they were to have a chance of moving forward, he had to go through with this. 'That now I know you're not my biological father, you think I don't see you as my father any more.'

'Uh-huh.'

Alex sighed. 'Dad, has anyone ever told you how bloody difficult you can be?'

Will stared at him. 'You just called me "Dad".'

'What else am I going to call you? That's who you've been for the last thirty-five years,' Alex pointed out.

'So you still think of me like that?'

'Of course I do,' Alex said. 'The only thing that's changed is a bit of genetic coding that I didn't know about before, and that doesn't make any diff...' He broke off and grimaced. 'Well, I guess it does make a difference if I've inherited *that* gene, but otherwise it doesn't change the fact that you're the one who taught me to kick a football, swim, and ride a bike, and yelled at me so I knuckled down to study properly for my exams. You're my dad. Always have been, always will be.'

Will looked hugely relieved. 'I'm glad.'

'So you really thought I'd put a total stranger above you in my life? Why didn't you say something before?' Alex asked.

'You had enough to deal with, without fussing about my feelings. Anyway, *you* could've said something,' Will pointed out.

'I am now.'

Will raised an eyebrow. 'I thought they were supposed to teach you personal skills as part of your doctor training nowadays?'

Alex laughed. 'If you were a mum with a complicated pregnancy, you'd think my bedside manner was perfect.'

'Whereas I'm a sixty-three-year-old retired orthopod. And, from what I can see, your bedside manner is no better than mine.'

'Like father, like son,' Alex said quietly. 'I'm not so good with words outside work, but I'm learning to talk things over.'

Will looked thoughtful. 'Then I should make the effort and join you.'

'What about Mum?' Alex asked.

Will sighed. 'I'm trying, Alex. The stupid thing is, if

she'd told me the truth when she was pregnant, it wouldn't have mattered. It's the fact that she kept it from me for all those years that upset me most. It made me wonder what else she hadn't told me. And, even though she says there isn't anything, it's so easy to misread things.'

Alex was truly shocked. 'You think she had other affairs?'

Will blew out a breath. 'I'll be honest with you. It did cross my mind. I'm not proud of myself—I actually asked her, and I could see how much I hurt her by doubting her. There wasn't anyone else. Stephen just caught her at a bad time, when she was very unhappy. We weren't getting on well and I'd just gone off to Edinburgh on secondment. I didn't talk it over properly with her first and just expected her to get on with it. So it's not all her fault.'

Before his mother's shock news, Alex had always looked up to his parents as an example of the perfect marriage—two people who'd loved each other for decades. When so many marriages seemed to collapse after five minutes, his parents' marriage had made Alex believe that love could really last. Learning that he was the product of an affair had really floored him. And now it looked as if his parents' marriage was going to crumble.

'Are you thinking about a divorce?' he asked.

Will grimaced. 'I love your mother. Always have. And I think she loves me. But we're both treading on eggshells all the time, and I don't really know how to stop it.'

'Go to counselling?' Alex suggested. 'Talk to someone who isn't involved and won't judge or take sides?'

Will pulled a face. 'I hate the idea of it, having someone prying in my head. But if that's what it takes to sort things out between your mother and me, I guess I'm going to have to man up and do it. Because I don't want to throw away thirty-seven years like that.' He looked at Alex. 'As we're bringing everything into the open, you should know that your mother thinks you're punishing her.'

Alex frowned. 'Punishing her? How?'

'By not coming home very often and—more importantly—by refusing to take the test to find out if you've got the faulty gene.'

'I'm not punishing her.' Alex sighed. 'The reason I haven't come home is because I thought my being around would make things worse between you. And as for the test, what if it turns out to be positive? She'll blame herself and break her heart over it. At least this way, not knowing, she can't blame herself.'

'Actually, uncertainty,' Will said quietly, 'is what causes the most problems for patients.'

'I'm nobody's patient.'

'I know.' He sighed. 'And you're an adult. It's your choice.'

'Knowing one way or another isn't going to make any difference,' Alex said. 'You know as well as I do that there isn't a cure for Huntington's and there aren't any lifestyle changes that would stave it off or stop it progressing.'

'Have you talked it over with your fr—your colleague?' Will corrected himself.

'Sort of. She says the only person who can make the decision is me, and only when I'm ready to face the results.' He paused. 'Dad—if it was you, would you want to find out that in twenty years' time your quality of life will be next to nothing? That you won't be able to control all your movements, you'll become too clumsy and forgetful to be able to do the job you love, you'll have mood swings and be impossible to live with, and you'll have difficulty swallowing and even speaking? That you'll need help to do the simplest of tasks, you'll get to the point where you need full nursing care, and—worst of all—you'll just be a burden to everyone around you, to the point where they won't be able to remember the good times but just the sheer grinding drudgery of life as a carer?'

'I don't know,' Will said. 'I plan things. So I think that yes, I probably would want to know one way or the other. If the test was negative, then fine. If it was positive, then at least I'd be spared the uncertainty, the worry that every time I spill my coffee it might be the first sign of a neurodegenerative disease instead of being just a silly little thing that happens to everyone. I'd want to be able to plan my own care, to warn my family what to expect as the disease progresses and most of all to make sure they know I love them while I'm still capable of telling them so.' He paused. 'I don't say it often enough, Alex, but I love you. I've loved you since the moment I first held you in the delivery suite. And just because I'm not your real dad—'

'Oh, but you *are* my real dad,' Alex cut in. 'It takes more than a random sperm to make a father. You've always been there for me.' Unlike Stephen. 'And I'm sorry I've let you down this year.'

Will shook his head. 'You haven't let me down. It's been difficult for all of us.'

'I wish Mum had never met Stephen.'

'But then,' Will said, 'we wouldn't have had you. And that's the bit I'll never regret.'

Will's face was bright with sincerity, and it put a huge lump in Alex's throat. 'Thanks, Dad.'

'Come home soon,' Will said. 'Bring your colleague.'

'She's strictly my colleague, Dad. I'm not in the right place for it to be anything else.'

'Pity.'

Yes, it was. The more he got to know Dani, the more he liked her. It wasn't just the physical side of things either—he liked her for herself. But he wouldn't ask her to take on the enormity of his burden, just as he'd made sure that Lara was free to find someone who'd give her the love and happiness she deserved.

Will finished his pint, then gave Alex a hug. 'I mean it. Come home soon.'

'I will,' Alex promised.

Even though it was a Saturday evening and Alex was pretty sure that Dani's social diary was full to the brim, he called her on the way back from the pub.

'Hey. Are you at home?'

'Yes. Why?'

'Are you busy, or can I pop in and see you for a minute?'

'Of course you can,' she said. 'Is something wrong?'

'No. I just wanted to talk to you about something.'

'OK. I'm around all evening.'

'See you in a bit.'

Alex called in to the supermarket to get some nice flowers—even if one of the high-end florists had been open, he was pretty sure that Dani would prefer something a little less flashy and over-the-top—then headed for her flat.

She looked taken aback when she opened the door to him and he handed her the flowers. 'What are these for?'

'To say thanks,' he said.

She frowned. 'For what?' Then she shook herself. 'Come in and tell me. Coffee, tea, wine or water?'

'Coffee would be great, thanks.' He followed her into the kitchen and tried not to think about how it had felt to kiss her there.

Dani put the kettle on and shook grounds into her cafetière, then put the flowers in water. 'These are really lovely—thank you.'

'It's the least I could do. You know your pep talk? Well, I met my dad for a pint tonight. We talked. *Really* talked.'

'And?'

'You were right.' And he still couldn't believe how wrong he'd been. 'It wasn't that seeing me rubbed his nose in it. He thought I didn't see him as my dad any more.'

'So things are better between you now?' she asked.

'Yes. If it hadn't been for you then I would never even have talked to him about it.'

'Being bossy has its benefits,' she said with a grin.

He wanted to hug her.

But he could also remember what it felt like to hold her properly. To carry her to her bed. And, much as he wanted to repeat it, in the circumstances it really wasn't fair.

'Not joining me in coffee?' he asked instead when she only made one mug of coffee and then filled a glass with cold water.

'I'm on a health kick, getting ready for the walking cast to be off and my foot to be officially in rehab,' she said. 'Plus it's a bit hypocritical of me to bang on to Haze about the importance of hydration if I don't bother doing it myself.'

'Haze—that's Hayley in the emergency department, right?' he checked.

'Yes. The one who's running for me. Actually, it was my evening to train with her tonight. I'd just got back when you called.'

'You're training with her?' He gave her foot a pointed look.

'As in bossing her about. Sitting on a gym ball next to her treadmill in the gym and directing her when to change the incline or the speed, and distracting her to keep her going through the tough bits. Sam's doing all the proper outdoor stuff with her.'

'Sam?'

'He's one of the registrars in the emergency department. He's saved me from sitting on a bench and freezing my backside off while Haze does a practice run round the park.'

'Got you. So if he's training, too, does that mean he's running the race as well?' Alex asked.

'No. Sam joined Muswell Hill after the closing date for the race. He's just helping out because he's a runner and—well, it's a way of him getting to know people when he's still new to the team.'

'Uh-huh. So do you have a sponsor form, or are you raising the money online?'

'Both.'

He grabbed his wallet, emptied out all the notes and handed them to her. 'Sponsor money.'

Her beautiful dark eyes widened. 'I can't accept that.'

'It's for equipment for our department so yes, you can,' he corrected. 'Plus you're the one who's having this Year of Saying Yes. So, under those rules, surely you have to say yes?'

'That,' she said, 'is very cheeky of you. But thank you.' She opened a drawer, took a form and a pen from a cardboard folder and handed them to him. 'Actually, I'll be cheeky now. Would you mind gift aiding it, so we can reclaim the tax?'

'No problem.' He filled in the relevant bits of the form and signed it.

'Thank you. I appreciate it.' She put the form back in the folder, along with the money.

'So how's the training going?' he asked.

'Good. Haze absolutely hates running, so she's doing an amazing job. Without her, I would've had to give the sponsorship money back.'

'She seems nice,' Alex said.

'She is. We met on our first day at university. Her room was next door to mine. I had hot chocolate, she had choc-chip cookies, we were both feeling incredibly homesick, and we cried all over each other,' Dani said. 'We've been best friends ever since.'

Pretty much like the way he'd met his own best friend. Except Alex had pushed Tom away. Maybe it was time to repair some bridges there, like the one he'd just repaired with his father. Maybe he should ring Tom.

Funny how Danielle Owens had made such a huge difference to his life.

And he damped down the regrets before they had a chance to strike hold.

CHAPTER FIVE

OVER THE NEXT couple of weeks, Dani managed to persuade Alex to join her for lunch almost every day with a couple of other people from the ward, and she was pleased to see that he started relaxing with the team enough to drop his aloofness. She was still aware of the slight distance he kept between himself and his colleagues, but his working relationship with the rest of the team was so much better than it had been.

She didn't manage to persuade him to take part in the pub quiz against the emergency department, but he had at least paid his deposit for his place at the ward's Christmas meal and was on the brink of agreeing to go to the team's pizza and bowling night later in the month.

On the last Sunday of October, Dani headed down to Alexandra Park with Hayley and Sam, getting Hayley set up with her numbered bib and the electronic tag for her shoe that would record her time. She noticed the glances between Hayley and Sam; it looked to her as if they were sorting out their differences and Hayley was starting to accept the fact that Sam's job meant he put himself in danger from time to time. So maybe, just maybe, they would move on together. Find happiness.

Although Dani was really pleased for her best friend,

because Hayley really deserved to find love again, part of her was quietly envious. How long was it since she'd last felt loved and cherished?

She pushed the thought away. She was *not* going to let Leo spoil the rest of her life. She'd learned the hard way that it was pointless loving someone who wouldn't or couldn't love you back. And today was a good day. The hated walking cast was finally gone and she could start to rehab her foot properly. She'd focus on that.

'Are you OK, Dani?' Sam asked, looking concerned, when they were standing by the barrier next to the runners.

'I'm fine,' she lied with a smile. Actually, she wasn't feeling that great. Maybe she was coming down with something, and that was why her mood had dipped today.

She chatted to Sam as they waited for Hayley to come past them at the end of her first lap, and then they walked further down to the finish line. Dani could see Hayley starting to flag, but then Hayley looked up and saw Dani and Sam cheering her on, and it seemed to give her a last boost.

Once Hayley was over the finish line, Dani and Sam swept her into a joint hug. 'You're wonderful,' Dani said. 'Because of you, we've raised a ton of money for the new equipment for the ward.'

'People donated because of you,' Hayley reminded her.

'But you're the one who actually ran the race so we could keep the sponsor money.' Dani hugged her hard. 'Thank you so much.'

Hayley hugged her back and then hugged Sam. 'Thank you both. I couldn't have done it without you training with me.'

Sam picked her up, swung her round and kissed her.

'You did brilliantly. I'm so proud of you.' Then he set Hayley back on her feet and rested his forehead against hers. 'Sorry. I know we were keeping this between us, but I kind of assumed Dani would know as she's your best friend.'

Yeah. Dani knew. It radiated out of the pair of them. 'She'd kept it sort of quiet, but I'd already guessed from the way you two look at each other,' Dani said with a smile, 'and it's a good thing.' It was. She was genuinely pleased for them.

But part of her couldn't help wishing that it had been different between her and Alex. That he would've been here with them today, hugging her and kissing her and looking at her as if she made his world feel full of sunshine, the way that Sam looked at Hayley.

And what kind of miserable cow was she, to envy her best friend's happiness?

She and Alex had agreed to be friends, so it was pointless wishing it could be otherwise. The best thing she could do now was to join a dating site or something and find someone she could have some fun with.

'Come on, let's go get your time,' Sam said to Hayley, 'and then I'm taking you both out for refuelling.'

Even though Dani really didn't fancy coffee and pastries—which had to be absolute proof that she was going down with a bug—she didn't want to spoil Hayley's joy at not only running the race but achieving a personal best time, too, so she joined them at the café.

But on the way back to her flat Dani realised what had been subconsciously nagging at her for the last day or so.

Her period was nearly two weeks late.

OK. Maybe it was stress—she'd been busy at work, and there was the whole thing about breaking her foot;

although she'd tried to stay cheerful about it, she'd felt hampered and miserable about not being able to do the kind of exercise she loved. Yes, she'd actually had sex with someone in the last month, but given the circumstances Alex had been very careful indeed about contraception. They'd used protection.

On the other hand, she was an obstetrician and she knew from experience that the only contraception that was one hundred per cent reliable was abstinence. How many mums had she seen in her career who'd had a hard time adjusting to an unexpected pregnancy?

She pushed the thought away. She was just a bit under the weather, that was all. Maybe she was going down with a bug. It was completely ridiculous to think that the way she felt could be due to being pregnant.

But she still couldn't shift the idea. If another woman had described the symptoms to her, she would've asked about the possibility of pregnancy: going off coffee, feeling slightly sick, having tender breasts.

Or maybe she was panicking over nothing, blowing this whole thing out of proportion. Her breasts were probably a bit tender simply because her period was due any day now, and the rest of the symptoms were all just in her head.

In the end, instead of going straight home, she called in to a supermarket and bought a pregnancy test. She'd do the test, see for herself that the result was negative, and then she could put this crazy notion completely out of her head. Of course she wasn't pregnant.

Though, once she got home, she found herself sitting on the loo with the test stick in her hand and she just couldn't produce any urine at all.

Oh, for pity's sake. How stupid and pathetic was this?

After three big glasses of water and pacing up and down her flat for ten minutes, she tried again. This time, to her relief, she managed to get a urine sample; she replaced the cap and laid the test stick flat on the bathroom sink while she washed her hands. She'd bought one of the newest digital tests, so there would be no chance of misinterpreting the result. In three minutes' time, she'd know for sure. There was even a little line along the bottom of the screen, showing that the test was working; as each minute passed, another segment of the line disappeared. There would be no mistake here.

She swallowed hard as she watched the last segment. One minute to go. She'd never known the seconds tick by so slowly before. But everything was going to be all right. The screen would say say 'not pregnant' in big black letters and she could laugh the whole thing off as the product of an overactive imagination.

She looked away for a second.

And then she looked at the screen and it felt as if her heart had stopped.

Instead of the reassurance she'd expected, there was a single word.

Pregnant.

She blinked hard. She had to be seeing things. Panicking over nothing.

But when she looked again, the word was still there. On its own. No reassuring 'not' had appeared above it.

Pregnant.

What the hell was she going to do?

She splashed her face with water, and looked at the screen again. No change. Still defiantly *pregnant*.

Funny. A year ago, she would've been overjoyed. Amazed, given that she and Leo had hardly made love any more, but overjoyed. She'd got to the stage where delivering babies wasn't quite enough for her, and she'd wanted a child of her own. To make a family, with her husband. When she'd broached the subject to Leo, he'd told her that he wasn't ready—that he wanted to notch up another promotion before he felt comfortable trying for a family, and all his time was taken up working for the promotion. So she'd damped down the longing for a baby and just carried on as usual.

Except Leo had been carrying on, too. In a different sense of the phrase. With someone else. And he'd given his lover the baby that he'd refused to give his wife.

She dragged in a breath. Here she was, a year later, still damping down the fact that she wanted a baby—she hadn't even admitted that bit to Hayley.

And now she was unexpectedly pregnant, by a man she barely knew.

And she didn't have a clue what to do next.

She wasn't sure if she was pleased, terrified, or what. Everything suddenly seemed topsy-turvy. Weren't accidental pregnancies meant to happen to careless teenagers who didn't think of the consequences, not thirty-two-year-old obstetricians who'd been careful with contraception?

'Danielle Owen, stop being such a wimp,' she told herself sternly. 'You're Dr Organised, the one everyone comes to for advice, remember?'

Maybe that was the way forward: to pretend it was

happening to someone else. What would she advise someone else to do, in her shoes?

She sat down at her kitchen table with a pad and a
pen to make a list.

Talk to the father.

Given that they weren't a couple, and their night together had been a one-off, this conversation would've
been awkward in any case. But what was going to make
it so much worse was the Huntington's situation. If Alex
hadn't inherited the faulty gene, he couldn't pass it on.
But if he had inherited the faulty gene, there was a fifty
per cent chance that he'd passed it to the baby. The only
way of knowing for sure was to do a test—and she knew
how strongly he felt about not doing the test.

Maybe that conversation shouldn't be the first one.

She wrote down the next item on her list.

Talk to your best friend.

Except right now Dani was pretty sure that Hayley
was happy for the first time in well over a year, and she
really didn't want to pile her worries onto her best friend
and wreck that happiness. Hayley had had a horrible
time, losing her fiancé in the most tragic circumstances—
Evan, as a firefighter, had been killed trying to rescue
someone from a fire. She deserved to enjoy every bit of
happiness, now she had the chance, instead of worrying
about Dani's situation.

Dani put a line through that option.

Talk to your GP.

Again, it was a conversation that she would need to have at some point in the next couple of weeks. But this was Sunday afternoon, well outside normal surgery appointment times. So that call wasn't going to be top of her list either.

Talk to your parents.

It was a possibility. Dani knew her parents would support her. But right now they were in Scotland, visiting her grandparents. They'd be left worrying about her, and that wasn't fair—not when they were hundreds of miles away and it would be hard for them to get to her. She struck a line through that option, too.

Which left her with option one.

Talk to the father.

Discussing the situation with Alex.

She'd have to think very, very carefully about how she broke the news to him. And she really didn't know enough about Huntington's to have that conversation.

Well, OK. Lack of knowledge. That was something she could fix. She grabbed her laptop and went looking for information.

An hour's research left her drained and miserable. Alex hadn't been exaggerating. There wasn't a cure, there was nothing you could do to stave off the disease, and there was no real way of predicting when you'd start to get symptoms. But while she'd been doing the research she'd also thought of someone else she could talk to about the situation. Emma, who'd trained with her as a student and had gone on to specialise in IVF and genetics. And, more importantly, Emma worked at a different hospital, so there was no chance of anyone seeing them together, jumping to conclusions and gossiping—which meant there was no chance of Alex hearing something through the hospital grapevine and leaping to his own conclusions before she'd had a chance to talk to him.

She grabbed her phone and called Emma.

Given the way her luck seemed to be running that day, she wasn't too surprised when her call went through to voicemail. She sighed inwardly and left a message on the answering service, trying hard to sound bright and cheerful. 'Hi, Em. It's Dani. I was wondering if I could pick your brains about something over a pizza some time in the next few days? Look forward to hearing from you.'

Which gave her the rest of the afternoon to brood, clean her flat, and try to work out how on earth she was going to break the news to Alex.

She was still no nearer to any kind of solution when her phone rang.

'Hey, Dani! It's Em. Sorry I missed your call earlier. I'd put my phone on silent because I was babysitting my niece this afternoon and she'd actually gone to sleep,' Emma said.

'No worries. Thanks for calling back,' Dani said.

'So what do you want to pick my brains about?'

'Some advice for a patient about a genetic matter.'

'*My* advice?' Emma sounded surprised. 'Wouldn't you be better off talking to the genetic team at Muswell Hill, given that she's your patient?'

'It's a bit of a sensitive situation,' Dani hedged.

'Ah—in that case I'm guessing she works with you and she doesn't want anyone else to know about the pregnancy yet.'

It was close enough not to feel like a complete lie. 'Yes.'

'OK. Let's talk. Are you free tonight?'

Dani felt the tears of relief well up and blinked them away. 'Yes—yes, I am.'

'Great. Let's go to Luigi's. Meet you there at half seven?'

'Brilliant. And it's my shout,' Dani said, 'as I'm making you work for your supper.'

Emma laughed. 'You're on. See you later.'

At the Italian restaurant, Emma looked pointedly at Dani's foot. 'So the evil boot is off at last?'

'It is indeed. And Haze ran in my place this morning and raised a ton of money towards the scanner,' Dani said with a smile. 'Thanks for your donation, by the way.'

'My pleasure, and good for Haze. You should've brought her along tonight. I haven't seen her for ages and it'd be good to catch up,' Emma said.

'I kind of need to keep this confidential,' Dani said.

'I can't imagine Haze gossiping, but I guess you made a promise to your colleague,' Emma said with a shrug. 'Let's order, then you can tell me all about it.'

Once they'd ordered—and Dani claimed to be drinking water only as part of a health kick, now she could rehab her no longer broken foot—Emma took a swig of her red wine. 'So tell me about your friend and the genetic stuff.'

'The mum's in the early stages of pregnancy—but she's worried because the dad might have Huntington's,' Dani said.

'Might? So he hasn't actually had the test yet?' Emma asked.

Dani shook her head. 'Though one of his parents died

from it, so she knows there's a fifty per cent chance he's inherited the faulty gene.'

'Huntington's. That's a fault on chromosome four,' Emma said thoughtfully. 'So if he's clear, the baby's fine. If he's not, the baby has a fifty per cent chance of inheriting it.'

Dani already knew that, and it scared her spitless. What if the test showed that the baby was in the wrong side of that fifty per cent? Could she go ahead and have a child, knowing that the baby had inherited a neurodegenerative disorder that didn't have a cure? And, worse, that the child would probably die in early middle age, needing full nursing care and having no real quality of life for the last few years? On the other hand, she hated the idea of having a termination. Her job as a doctor was to protect life.

Whatever option she took, the baby would lose.

And she wasn't sure she could live with that kind of guilt.

She swallowed hard. 'So what are my friend's options?'

'She really needs to get her partner to have the test,' Emma said, 'and then if it's positive we can test the baby.'

There were two problems there, Dani thought. For a start, Alex wasn't her partner. She could handle that—some of her friends were single parents, and she knew she'd have support from her family and friends—but the second problem was the really tricky one. And that was where she really hoped Emma could give her some practical suggestions. 'The thing is, he doesn't actually want to have the test.'

'Ah.' Emma grimaced. 'That makes things a bit more difficult. You said she was in the early stages of pregnancy—how early?'

'Very early days. She did the test this week when she realised she was a couple of weeks late. So I guess that'd be roughly six weeks since her LMP.'

'OK. So right now she's in a place where she knows nothing. There's a fifty-fifty chance he has the faulty gene. If he does have it, there's a fifty-fifty chance the baby has inherited it. Which works out to a one in four chance for the baby having it. And if you're the one facing that risk, it's scary stuff indeed.' She blew out a breath. 'Your poor friend must be worried sick.'

'Uh-huh.' That was putting it mildly. This morning, Dani had thought she was going down with a bug. Right now, she knew for definite that she was pregnant and there were horrible odds that the baby had inherited the neurodegenerative disease that had killed Alex's father. 'Is it possible to test the baby without the dad needing to have the test?'

'In theory, yes. We can do CVS at some point between ten and fourteen weeks,' Emma said.

Chorionic villi sampling or CVS was where a small sample of the placenta was taken via a needle through the abdomen; as an obstetrician Dani knew that the placenta contained the same genetic material as the baby, so the lab could test the placental samples and be sure that the result would be the same as if they'd taken cells from the baby.

'But, apart from the one per cent risk of CVS causing a miscarriage,' Emma said, 'that kind of testing is a real ethical minefield. For a start, it breaches the father's rights, because if the baby's positive then it means he's positive—he'll know without having the test himself. Plus the baby can't give consent to testing.'

'So you can't actually do the test in practice?' Dani asked.

'We can do the test,' Emma said. 'But under the code of ethics we're bound by, the mum would have to sign papers before we did the CVS, agreeing to a termination if the results show that the baby has Huntington's.'

'Seriously?' Dani looked at her friend, totally shocked.

'Seriously, and it's a horrible decision to have to make,' Emma said. 'It's a shame her GP had didn't send her for genetic counselling before they started trying for a baby, because she could've been given a few more options to help avoid the baby inheriting Huntington's. She could've had pre-implantation genetic diagnosis. That's the area I'm working in at the moment. It means if a couple has a known genetic problem between them—say one of them has sickle cell disease—they can have IVF. We'll wait for two or three days until the embryo has divided into eight cells, then we'll take one of those cells from the embryo and check to see if it contains the gene that causes the problem. If it doesn't, then we know the baby can't inherit the condition and we can transfer the embryo to the mother's womb; then the IVF process continues as normal.'

Meaning that if Alex had Huntington's, with PGD his baby wouldn't inherit the condition.

She realised that Emma was waiting for her to say something. OK. She'd respond as a fellow doctor, not as a mum-to-be. 'It's pretty amazing that you can run those kinds of tests from a single cell.'

'I know. That's why I'm specialising in it,' Emma said. 'I love the idea of being able to help people avoid their baby inheriting a condition that's made them lose people too early in their family—people with a family history of

Duchenne's muscular dystrophy, say, or haemophilia. I know it's kind of like playing God, but it's so nice to be able to take away the worry and the heartache. To make a real difference to my patients. A parent with sickle cell who has PGD will know their child definitely won't have to suffer the same kind of pain they've gone through.'

'I get that,' Dani said. 'And that would definitely be an option for my friend in the future.' For Alex, maybe. Because their one night wasn't going to be repeated. 'Except I don't think this baby was actually planned.'

'You and I both know that, even if they were super-super careful, the only guaranteed method of contraception is abstinence,' Emma said. 'Tell her not to beat herself up about it. It's not her fault.'

Wasn't it? Dani had already been thinking about that. How she'd been the one to proposition Alex, even though she'd known his situation. Then again, he'd been the one to kiss her, so maybe they were equally to blame.

'If your friend wants a confidential chat with me, I'm more than happy to talk to her. Give her my number—I won't pass anything on to your team,' Emma said. 'But that poor woman's got some really difficult decisions ahead of her. I hope she's got a good support team.' She smiled. 'Actually, I already know she does. She's got *you.*'

Yeah. Dani had herself. And she knew she was resilient. She'd got through Leo's betrayal and the divorce. She'd get through this, too.

Dani forced herself to smile back. 'Thanks for letting me pick your brain, Em. It's been really helpful.'

'Any time.'

Dani switched the conversation to something much lighter and tried to enjoy the rest of the evening as much as she could; but she knew was going to have to talk to

Alex about the situation. It would be easier if she had some idea how he was going to react, but she didn't know him well enough to have a single clue.

She'd need to be careful about this. Find the right words and the right time.

Somehow.

CHAPTER SIX

'CAN I HAVE a word?' Dani asked, leaning round the door of Alex's office.

'Sure. I assume it's about a patient so you need me to get the notes up?'

'No, actually,' she said. 'And I don't really want to talk here.'

Puzzled, he said, 'OK. Where and when?'

'Are you free this evening?' she asked.

'Yes.'

'OK. Say eight o'clock, my place?'

'Sure.'

It seemed a bit strange that she hadn't suggested dinner; for the last month Alex had been very aware of Dani's attempts to make him be more sociable. Maybe he was misinterpreting things, though he thought she'd looked worried about something. It was clear that she wasn't going to tell him what the problem was until later that evening, so he did what he'd learned to do ever since he'd found out the truth about Stephen—he compartmentalised it rather than brooding over it and just got on with the rest of his day.

And it turned out to be a good day, when he helped to deliver a breech baby. The bit he loved most about his job were those first few magical seconds of a new life, hearing the baby cry and seeing him open his eyes.

At eight on the dot, Alex rang Dani's doorbell.

'Come in. Wine, coffee, something cold?' she asked.

'No, I'm fine, thanks.'

She led him through to her living room and gestured to him to sit down.

'So what did you want to talk to me about?' he asked.

She swallowed hard. 'Um, there really isn't an easy way to put this.'

And she wasn't one for beating around the bush. One of the things he liked most about her was her straight-forwardness. Why was she suddenly being so awkward? 'Put what?'

She was silent for so long that he was about to repeat his question.

And then she said, her voice so soft that he could barely hear her, 'I'm pregnant.'

For a second, the world felt as if it had spun off its axis. No. He must have misheard. Dani couldn't be pregnant. She couldn't. They'd used a condom, and he'd been absolutely meticulous about putting it on and taking it off. There hadn't been a rip or tear. The condom hadn't burst. And, although he'd stayed overnight, they hadn't made love sleepily without a condom in the middle of the night. He'd just held her close and woken with her in his arms.

He stared at her. 'Can you repeat that?'

'I'm pregnant.'

So he hadn't misheard. 'How?'

She swallowed hard. 'We're both obstetricians. Surely we both know the mechanics of how a woman gets pregnant.' She dragged a hand through her hair. 'This wouldn't be an easy conversation in any situation, but with your family history it's a whole lot harder.'

She could say that again.

Dani was pregnant. And if Alex had inherited Huntington's from Stephen, that meant there was a fifty per cent chance that the baby could have inherited it from him—a situation he'd wanted to avoid so much that he'd broken his engagement to Lara over it.

'But we were careful,' he said, still trying to process the news.

'Yes. And we both know there's a tiny, tiny chance that any form of contraception will fail. A stupidly small chance if you're careful—which we were. But it happened.'

'You're absolutely sure you're pregnant?' he checked.

'Of course I'm sure!' Outrage flashed momentarily in her expression. 'I wouldn't have said anything to you without doing a test first. I did it yesterday afternoon. And it was one of the digital tests. There's no margin of error. The thing actually says the words on the screen so you don't have to work out whether that's a really faint blue line or your eyes are deceiving you. It was very definite. I'm pregnant.'

Pregnant. He couldn't quite get his head round this.

Though he knew without a doubt that the baby was his. Dani wasn't the sort to sleep around.

Of course he'd be there for her and the baby. Of course he'd accept his responsibilities. There was no question about that. And yet at the same time he was terrified that he'd passed the bad gene onto the baby. How could he possibly condemn his own child to the kind of death his biological father had had—to the one that he, too, might face?

It was all his fault. If he hadn't given in to that urge to kiss Dani, she wouldn't have suggested that he stay the night, and he wouldn't have carried her to her bed.

Instead, he'd followed Stephen's genes and been utterly selfish. He'd desperately wanted to take the warmth and comfort she'd offered, so he'd taken a risk. A calculated risk, one that meant she should've been protected from pregnancy—on average, two in a hundred women would become pregnant if they used condoms over the course of a year. Assuming that those hundred women had sex twice a week, that was two pregnancies out of ten thousand times of having sex. He and Dani had made love only once.

But once was all it took...

'Say something, will you?'

'What?' He blinked at her stupidly.

She glared at him. 'I've just told you I'm pregnant. And you've hardly said a word.'

'I don't know what to say.'

'So, what, you think it's all my fault?' Her glare hardened. 'Because I was the one who propositioned you, and I was the one with the condom that turned out to be faulty?'

Was that really what was going through her head? He thought she blamed her for it? 'No, of course I don't blame you. I could have said no and I didn't. It was both of us.'

She didn't look particularly mollified. 'So what happens now?'

He rubbed a hand across his face. 'Last time I was in this room with you, you said that it was up to me to do the test. That I didn't have to do it until I was ready.'

She narrowed her eyes at him. 'And?'

'And now, I admit, I feel as if my hand's been forced. Now it would be wrong of me not to do the test, because you need to know for the baby's sake.'

Her face looked pinched. 'There's a fifty per cent chance you have the gene, and if you do have it that means there's a fifty per cent chance you've passed it on. So that's a twenty five per cent chance the baby has it—one in four.'

He knew those odds only too well. He'd worked it out for himself months ago. 'That's why I broke off my engagement with Lara. Because she deserved the chance to have a family without having to worry about that.'

She rolled her eyes. 'There's more than one way to make a family, Alex, and you know it. Among other things there's IVF with donor sperm or PGD, plus there's fostering and adoption.'

He sighed. 'I know. I'm sorry. That's not what I meant.'

She folded her arms. 'This is why I'm talking to you about the situation. It's your baby, so you need to have a say in what happens now.'

'I don't really have a say,' he said. 'If I don't do the test for Huntington's, how else will you know if the baby's OK or not?'

'I can have the baby tested,' she said, 'but the baby can't give consent to the procedure.' There was the tiniest wobble in her voice, telling him just how upset she was about the situation. 'And that means I have to sign papers before they do the test, agreeing to have a termination if the test results come back positive.'

He looked at her, utterly shocked. 'Seriously?'

She nodded. 'I didn't know that until yesterday. I talked to a friend I trained with, who specialises in genetics and IVF. She explained it all to me. She works in a different hospital, so if anybody did see us by chance or overheard what we said, nobody's going to connect our conversation with you and me.'

He felt his eyes widen. 'Hang on. You told her about us?'

'No. I told her about the situation, and she assumed it was a friend who was affected. I didn't correct her.' She dragged in a deep breath. 'But it's such a mess, Alex. If I have the baby tested, then it also breaches your rights. Because if the results mean I have to have a termination, then you'll know you definitely have Huntington's because there's no trace of it in my family history. And that isn't fair, because you haven't agreed to take a test.'

He looked at her. 'But if the baby doesn't have Huntington's, that still doesn't mean I'm clear. It might be that I have the faulty gene but on this occasion I didn't pass it on.'

'Right now, the baby has a one in four chance of having Huntington's,' she said. 'And I really don't like those odds.'

He knew he had to do the right thing, even though it tied him up in knots because he hadn't wanted to know for definite whether he had Huntington's. He'd wanted to enjoy however much life he had left without feeling as if he had an axe hanging over his head. Now he had no choice. 'OK. I'll do the test,' he said.

'And what if you're positive?'

'Then we'll get the baby tested. It'll have to be through CVS.' He paused. Even though he could work it out for himself—they'd had sex four weeks ago—he needed to ask. 'Exactly how pregnant are you?'

'My LMP was six weeks ago,' she said.

'So I need to get the test results back within the next

five to eight weeks, to hit the right window if the baby has to be tested.' And that could open up a whole new can of worms. 'If the baby tests positive, we have a decision to make. Do we go ahead and have the baby, knowing that a cure for Huntington's might not be available in my lifetime, let alone the child's? Or do we...?' He stopped, not wanting to voice it.

'Terminate the pregnancy,' she finished, 'because otherwise we're condemning a child to an incurable neurodegenerative condition?' Her face was anguished. 'I don't know. Either way, we lose.'

'It's a one in four chance we'll have to have that conversation.'

'They're huge odds, Alex. *Huge*.'

He could see the panic in her eyes. 'I know.'

'And we ended up the wrong side of the tiny odds that the condom wouldn't work. How do we know we won't end up the wrong side of such massive odds as these ones?'

He could see in her face that she was torn apart by this. He was feeling shell-shocked by the possibilities himself, and he'd only known for a few minutes; she'd had a day or so to think about the situation, run through the options and worry about them even more.

'How are you doing?' he asked carefully.

'I'm holding it together at work, but inside I'm a mess,' she admitted. 'I wasn't expecting this.'

Neither had he.

'And I can't see a way forward. Anything we do will be wrong.' She dragged in a breath. 'You don't want children.'

'I didn't.' Not since he'd discovered the truth about his parentage. Before then, he'd thought he was ready to start trying for a baby on his honeymoon. Afterwards, the situation had changed. Become much bleaker.

He and Dani hadn't discussed it, so he had no idea of her views on the subject. 'Do you want children?' he asked.

'I did. Which was why it hurt so much that Leo left me for the other woman—that she was carrying his baby.' She looked away. 'Last year, at the beginning of summer, I told him I wanted a baby. He said he wasn't ready to start a family. That he was working towards a promotion and he wanted to get that sorted out before we started try-ing for a baby. And all the time he was sleeping with the other woman. Which I guess was why he wasn't sleeping with me—though I thought he wasn't sleeping with me because he was stressed about work and maybe because he was scared that I'd do something stupid to force his hand, like forget to take the Pill.'

Alex wasn't sure what shocked him most—the sheer selfishness of her ex's behaviour, or the way he'd tried to make Dani feel that it was her fault. 'You wouldn't do anything I've that. You're not devious,' he said.

'Thank you.'

She looked relieved that he believed in her integrity. But what she'd just told him made things that much more complicated. She'd wanted a baby and her ex had denied her that opportunity. He'd rubbed salt in the wounds by having a baby with someone else. And now Dani was pregnant—albeit it was unplanned. Having to face the possibility of a termination, when she'd so wanted a child, must be torture.

Neither of them had signed up for this.

But no way was he going to start a relationship where he could end up being a burden to his partner. He wasn't selfish like his biological father. He'd been brought up by a kind, decent man, and he'd do the right thing by Dani and their baby.

He knew what he needed to do right now. She looked lonely and lost and defeated. He needed to reassure her. Hold her close, like she'd held him close when he'd felt lonely and lost and defeated. So he stood up, went over to her chair, scooped her up and sat down in her place, settling her on his lap with his arms wrapped round her. 'Neither of us bargained for this,' he said. 'Neither of us has a clue what's going to happen or what we do next. But I do know one thing: I'm not going to walk away from my responsibilities. I'll be there for you and the baby.'

Tears formed in her eyes. 'How? We're not even a couple.'

'And we can't be, if I have Huntington's. That's not negotiable.' He knew he was being stubborn and difficult, but he just couldn't budge on that point. It was too important.

'Alex, it could be years and years before you start to get symptoms. In that time, researchers could find a cure, or at least a way to manage the condition or slow it down.'

'They can manage some of the symptoms now,' he said dryly. 'But you have to be realistic. Most people get forty years of good health before they start getting symptoms. I'm thirty-five. That gives me five years before it starts, Dani. Supposing I have it but I didn't pass it on to the baby, and we go ahead with the pregnancy—the baby won't even have started school by the time I start getting symptoms.'

'*If* you have it,' she said. 'And that's a fifty-fifty chance.'

'You said it yourself: the risk of the baby having it is

huge, and my risk is twice as high,' he said softly. 'And you need to be realistic about what could happen. I know this is all going to sound really bleak, but it needs facing.' And the best way for her to do that was to hear directly it from him. 'If Stephen passed the faulty gene to me, then I'll need medication for mood swings and depression. I'll need medication to manage involuntary movements, and occupational therapy to help me as my motor skills decline. I'll need help managing my food, from turning everything into soup to eventually needing a PEG feed. And then there's communication—speech difficulties are often one of the first things to occur, and the cognitive problems vary from moment to moment. I might be able to make an articulate request to you over breakfast, and then five minutes later I won't be able to repeat it. I won't have the words or anything approaching them. It's going to be frustrating, both for me and anyone trying to communicate with me, and with the mood difficulties as well I might not be able to control an aggressive response,' he warned.

'Was that what it was like for Stephen?' she asked.

Alex nodded. 'His partner was really kind. He was at the stage where he couldn't communicate very well and Catriona really helped me to talk to him. But I could see the strain on her, Dani. She loved him enough to stay, but seeing him decline a little bit more every single day and not being able to do anything to stop it—it was killing her.' He blew out a breath. 'The first time I saw Stephen, he could only really communicate with me via a picture board. The second time, he was having a good day and could manage a few words. But by the time I met him he needed full nursing care, Dani. He needed someone to wash him and dress him and feed him. He needed someone to lift him into a chair and push him around. He couldn't do a single thing for himself. And I would really, *really* hate to be that helpless. To put that kind of burden on the woman I love.' He held her close. 'What I'm saying is that there's a very real chance I don't have a future. But in the meantime I'm going to do my best to be there for you and the baby. I'll support you every step of the way for as long as I can.'

'What if the baby has Huntington's?' she asked.

'Right now we have a three in four chance of that not being the case.'

She didn't say it, but he could see it in her eyes. That risk wasn't anywhere near low enough.

'I'll ring my family doctor for an appointment tomorrow and I'll ask him to refer me for testing,' he said. 'And we're going to have to take this thing day by day. In a few weeks we might have to make a really horrible decision—but it'll be an informed decision and we'll talk it through and we'll make that decision *together*.' He leaned his forehead against hers. 'In another life I wouldn't be Stephen's biological son, I'd be Will's, and you and I would've planned this baby and both been thrilled about that pregnancy test. Or even if the baby wasn't planned we would've been able to share the joy, once we'd got over the shock of the news. I'm so sorry I've taken that joy away from you.'

She stroked his face. 'It's not your fault.'

Oh, but it was. 'I can't promise you that the future's going to be OK. Until we get the test results back, we won't know anything for sure,' he said. 'But I promise you I'll be there for you. Have you made an appointment yet with your GP?'

'No. I wanted to talk to you first.'

He nodded. 'If you want me to go with you, then I will.'

'No, it's fine.' She paused. 'If you want me to go with you to any of the genetics stuff, then I will. Because this goes both ways, Alex. You need as much support as I do.'

'I can't ask that of you.'

'You're not asking me. I'm telling you it's how it is. We're in this together.'

'That's the whole point. If I have Huntington's, I don't want to be a burden.'

'And if you don't?'

'Then...' He blew out a breath. 'Then it's a different matter.'

'We might be parents next summer.'

Which told him that for her, if the baby didn't have Huntington's, a termination wasn't an option. Though that was the way he felt, too. And now he knew he might be a father... He'd had a happy childhood. Idyllic, even. He'd grown up feeling loved, and he wanted the same for his own child. Yet how could he burden his child with having to watch his condition deteriorate, feeling help-less because there was nothing anyone could do to cure him? Wouldn't the baby be better off not knowing him?

'We might,' he said guardedly.

'And yet we barely know each other.'

Because the baby was an unexpected result from one night of comfort. They weren't in love with each other. They were attracted to each other, and he knew he liked her. What he wasn't sure about was what she thought about him. If she liked him, too, was that enough to make a solid relationship? And was that even what she wanted, or did she think they could work something out about the baby without having to live together and try to make a family?

'I can't promise you a future. Not right now,' he said. 'But we can do something about not knowing each other very well. I'll start. I'm an only child, my dad's a retired orthopod and my mum's a part-time coffee shop manageress, and they live on the other side of London.'

'I'm an only child, too,' she said. 'My mum's a history teacher and my dad's an accountant. They live in Surrey.' She paused. 'What else do you want to know?'

'If you weren't a doctor, what would you be?'

'A forensic scientist,' she said promptly, 'and I'd be one of the ones who does facial reconstructions from skeletons.'

He raised an eyebrow. 'That's very specific.'

'Mum's a history teacher,' she reminded him. 'I guess I inherited her love of history. When I was really little, I wanted to be an archaeologist. I can remember going up to Northumbria on holiday and seeing Hadrian's Wall and all the shoes and the letters at Vindolanda, and wondering what the people who lived there and wore the shoes and wrote the letters looked like. Then we went to Bamburgh and I was allowed to help the archaeologists in a little tiny bit of the dig. I didn't actually find anything, but I loved being able to help, and the archaeologist made a bit of a pet of me and let me handle things they'd just found.' She smiled. 'There was this little bronze hippo that fitted into my palm. It was so amazing. And I spent the rest of the holiday digging holes in the beach, trying to find a hippo of my own.'

He could just imagine it, and it charmed him.

And he had to damp down the sudden surge of longing at the idea of having a daughter who looked like Dani and who dug holes in the beach, trying to find lost treasure. He couldn't let himself bond with this baby. Not until they all knew where they stood.

'We used to go to the beach on holiday, too, when I was small; but it was always Cornwall and always involved building sandcastles,' he said. 'My granddad— mum's dad—loved military history, so they were never just your four basic buckets as towers with a little bit of wall in between. Our castles were always proper motte-and-bailey ones, with massive ramparts.' He smiled back at her. 'So I guess if I hadn't been a doctor I might've ended up being a builder, the sort who restores ancient buildings.'

'So there's one thing we have in common, then. A love of history.'

'And beaches.' He paused. 'Here's another one for you. Dog or cat?'

'Dog,' she said promptly. 'That was what I missed most about home when I was a student. I could talk to Mum and Dad, and send texts and photographs to their phones, but I really missed curling up with the dog when I was reading, or taking the dog out for a walk in the middle of a revision session to clear my head. I think that's why I started running in the park; it meant if I went to a park that had a dog area I could stop and chat to the owners and make a fuss of their dogs.' She wrinkled her nose. 'Which is possibly a bit wet of me.'

'No, it's not.' He liked this softer side of her. And he could just imagine her walking through the park, pushing a baby in a pram with a dog trotting alongside her. He shook himself mentally; he couldn't let himself go too far along with that fantasy and imagine what their baby might be like, not when they still might have a hideous decision to make. He'd already had to pull himself back from the idea of having a daughter. 'What sort of dog?'

'A liver and white English springer spaniel, like the ones I grew up with,' she said promptly. 'What about you? Dog or cat?'

'Dog,' he said.

'What sort?'

'Golden retriever. Ours was big and soft and fluffy, and she thought she was a lapdog. So you'd have thirty kilos of dog sprawled on your lap, whether you wanted it or not.' He smiled at the memory.

'She sounds gorgeous,' Dani said. 'What was her name?'

'Sally.'

'Ours was Oscar,' she said. 'Mum and Dad decided not to replace him when he died. But I think they'll get another when they retire. Maybe something smaller and less busy than a springer, but I think Mum really misses having a dog.'

It sounded as if Dani really missed having a dog, too. Had she had a dog with her husband, and her ex had claimed the dog as part of the divorce settlement? Alex didn't want to rub salt in her wounds by asking. But it was another bit of common ground between them. The more he was finding out about her, the more he thought they might be compatible. That they might have a chance of a future together.

'OK. We have history and dogs in common. And you're a runner.'

'From the way you just said that, I assume you're not?' she asked.

'Not outdoors,' he said. 'I run on a treadmill as a

warm-up at the gym, but I'd much rather do a weights session. It clears my head better.'

'Give me cardio any day. Dance aerobics, or a bit of plyo—I've really missed not being able to do burpees and jumping onto a box.' She smiled. 'So we're opposites on exercise. What else do you do for fun?'

He shrugged. 'Video games.'

She groaned. 'Don't tell me—the shoot-'em-up type?'

''Fraid so. You?'

'I'm not really a gamer. Though I do like sudoku puzzles. That's my usual vice before bed—three puzzles.'

'Mine's cryptic crosswords at the breakfast table,' he said. 'How about reading?

'Crime novels. Preferably ones with a forensic scientist, though there's a series I really love with a forensic archaeologist,' she said. 'You?'

'Thrillers. I'm a big Lee Child fan,' he said.

'So we're sort of on the same page,' she said with a smile.

He groaned. 'I'm ignoring that terrible pun.'

'What, not even the glimmer of a smile, Dr Morgan?' She batted her eyelashes at him.

Alex couldn't help smiling. In other circumstances, he would've kissed her. But he needed to keep a little distance between them. Even though that probably counted as shutting the stable door when the horse had run to the other side of the country, given that right now she was pregnant with his baby.

'I've got another one. Foodie or not bothered?' she asked.

'Eating out, I'd probably go for the foodie option,' he said. 'Eating in… I tend to cook very simple things that don't take a lot of time.' He looked at her. 'Though I noticed there's a shelf of cookery books in your kitchen, so I'm guessing you're foodie all the way.'

'Yup. I buy pomegranate molasses and actually use it,' she said. 'It's another thing that relaxed me when I was a student. Cooking something complicated, so I had to concentrate on that and let all the stuff I'd revised percolate into my brain, or else I'd burn dinner.' She grinned. 'It was great. I'd cook for everyone, we'd share the costs— and because I cooked it meant I could weasel out of doing the washing up. Wins all round.'

God, he really liked this woman.

Please let the test results be on their side. Because he was beginning to think that a life with Dani would be a very good life indeed.

'How about music?' he asked.

'Anything I can sing along to. You?'

'Indie rock,' he said. 'And blues guitar—Dad loves Peter Green, so I grew up with that and John Mayall playing in the car.'

'Sounds good. Another one for you: theatre or cinema?' she asked.

'Cinema, and I like suspense movies,' he said. 'You?'

'Both. Because I really, really like musicals, and they're awesome on stage.'

He looked at her, surprised. 'Seriously?'

'I'm word-perfect on *Mamma Mia* and *Grease*,' she said with a grin. 'Come with me next time one of them's on in the West End.'

'Can't. I'll be babysitting.' The words came out before he could stop them.

'Nice excuse,' she said. And then her smile faded as she clearly realised what he meant.

Babysitting their baby.

Except they didn't know whether their baby was going to have the bad gene. Or what they'd decide to do.

'How is this going to work out, Alex?' she asked.

He sighed. 'I haven't a clue. Once we've got the test results, we'll have a better idea of what our real options are. Until then, I guess we have to take it day by day and try not to think about it.' He stroked her face. 'All that stuff people say about a problem shared being a problem halved—that's not true. In our case it's a problem doubled.'

'I'm sorry.'

'It's not your fault. It's circumstances,' he said.

'It's not your fault either,' she said, as if guessing what was in his head.

He rather thought it was, but he wasn't in the mood to argue with her. Instead, he said, 'So are you getting any kind of early pregnancy symptoms?'

'Yes and no.' She wrinkled her nose. 'I was just feeling a bit under the weather. I thought maybe I was going down with a bug, because that was the only reason I could think of why I wouldn't fancy celebrating Hayley's run with coffee and pastries; but then on the way home it occurred to me that my period was two weeks late. With the build-up to the race, and being busy at work, and having that wretched walking cast, I'd completely lost track of the date. I did the pregnancy test to prove to myself that I was being totally unreasonable and ridiculous—that I was just late because I was busy and stressed.'

'Except you got the result you weren't expecting.'

'And I didn't know how you were going to react—especially in the circumstances.'

'I'm still getting used to the idea,' he said. And it was growing on him. Scarily so. He needed to keep the brakes on until he knew what the situation was with his own health. 'But you and the baby are my responsibility. That's not going to change.'

'I'm an adult. I'm responsible for myself,' she said.

'What I mean is I'll support you,' he said. 'Whatever decisions we have to make, we'll make them together.'

Dani liked the fact that Alex had immediately accepted his share of responsibility for the situation. The fact that he'd support her with the baby.

But what about them?

Did their relationship stand a chance? She knew he'd keep her stubbornly at a distance until he'd got the result back of his own genetic test—hadn't he broken his engagement for exactly that reason?—but, if the test was negative, did they have a chance to make a real go of things between them?

The more she got to know him, the more she liked him.

And she was definitely attracted to him.

But she'd made that mistake with Leo. She'd fallen in love with a man who'd fallen very quickly out of love with her. If she let herself fall for Alex, what if he ended up feeling the same way about her that Leo had? What if he thought she was bossy and impossible and couldn't stand to be with her? What if he tried to love her and couldn't—because the truth was that she was unloveable? She really didn't want to risk her heart again.

But everything was so mixed up.

As if he guessed at her thoughts, Alex stroked her face. 'Hey. We'll find a way through this. We just need to take it one day at a time.'

'One day at a time,' she echoed.

'I'm going to let you get some rest,' he said. 'And I'll see you tomorrow at work.'

'OK.' She wriggled off his lap. 'And thank you for being so—well, nice about it.'

'None of this is your fault,' he reminded her. 'It's circumstances. And we'll sort it out. Together.'

CHAPTER SEVEN

ALEX CALLED HIS family doctor first thing the next morning and was relieved to get an appointment for later that day, after his shift ended.

'So what can I do for you, Dr Morgan?' the doctor asked.

Alex explained the situation about his biological father having recently died from Huntington's. 'So I'd like you to refer me for testing, please.'

'Are you showing any symptoms of the disease?' the doctor asked.

'Not yet,' Alex said grimly. Though he'd been watching himself closely.

'Then we can offer you a pre-symptomatic predictive test. It'll show whether you've inherited the faulty gene, but we can't tell you when you'll start to show symptoms. You'll need to have genetic counselling before we do the test,' the doctor said.

'We can skip the counselling,' Alex said, 'because I already know I want to do the test.'

The doctor shook his head. 'When we do testing like this, it's always in conjunction with genetic counselling and it tends to be four appointments—one where they gather information, one with an in-depth discussion, one where they actually do the test, and one where you get the results. The whole process can take up to six months from start to finish.'

The problem was, he didn't have six months. 'I understand that,' Alex said carefully, 'but in this case I can't wait that long because there's a baby involved. We didn't plan the pregnancy; and, apart from it not being fair on any of us to have to wait that long for the results, we need to know as soon as possible in case we need to do a prenatal diagnosis test for the baby. I know it takes at least two weeks between the blood test and getting the result, because you need to check the CAG repeat in the DNA, but can we at least telescope the first three appointments together?'

The doctor looked thoughtful. 'I might be able to fast-track the counselling in this situation, but you will still need to see a counsellor.'

'I'll do whatever it takes,' Alex said, 'but I need an answer as fast as possible.'

'From what you've told me, you've known about the situation for a while and chose not to get tested before. The first thing the counsellor's going to ask is why.'

'Because knowing wouldn't make a difference,' Alex said. 'I can't change my lifestyle or take any kind of treatment to stave it off, so it felt a bit pointless having a test. But my circumstances have changed now, and so has my opinion—I need to know if I've inherited the faulty gene, for the baby's sake.'

'What support do you have?' the doctor asked.

A mother who was racked with guilt, a father who'd be there for him but Alex had a nasty feeling that it would put extra strain on his parents' relationship, and Dani: though it wasn't fair to burden her with his worries either.

Plus he'd deliberately pushed all his friends away. Which left him isolated, by his own choice. 'Loads,' he lied.

'Sometimes it can be helpful to talk to a stranger who's been through a similar situation,' the doctor said, 'so I'm going to give you details of a support group.'

'Thanks,' Alex said, though he was pretty sure he wouldn't use it. He could support himself.

'In the circumstances, I'll try to fast-track the testing, so hopefully you'll hear from the team some time this week.'

'Thank you,' Alex said quietly. 'I really appreciate it.'

'I hope this all works out the way you want it,' the doctor said.

So did Alex.

When he'd left the doctor's surgery, he called Dani.

'Hello?' she said, her voice croaky.

'Dani, it's Alex. Sorry, did I just wake you?'

'It's OK. I just nodded off when I got in from work, that's all.'

He felt guilty for waking her, but he'd wanted her to know the news as soon as possible. 'I've just seen my family doctor. He's referring me for the pre-symptomatic diagnostic test and counselling. In the circumstances, he's going to try and fast-track it and I should hopefully hear something this week.'

'That's good,' she said, still sounding sleepy.

'Since you've been asleep, have you eaten yet?'

'No. I was too tired to cook anything when I got in,' she admitted. 'I sat down, planning to have a power nap, but it went on for a bit longer than I expected. I'll probably just make myself some toast.'

Toast wasn't good enough nutrition for a pregnant

woman, in Alex's view. 'I can bring something round,' he said.

'Are you offering to cook dinner for me?' She sounded surprised.

'As obstetricians,' he said gently, 'we both know that one of the symptoms of early pregnancy is tiredness—and as an obstetrician I'd be happier to know that you're resting rather than rushing around. I'll pick something up from the supermarket. Apart from the obvious things to avoid, is there anything you'd rather not eat?'

'No. I'll eat pretty much anything, as long as it's fairly bland,' she said. 'And thank you.'

When he'd been to the supermarket, he went to Dani's flat. 'I bought ravioli—and I checked that the ricotta in it was pasteurised—and I've got a plain tomato sauce to go with it, plus some Parmesan and ciabatta bread. And I thought you might like some fresh strawberries and pineapple for pudding.'

Tears welled in her eyes. 'That's so lovely.' And then she blinked back the tears. 'Sorry. I'm being wet.'

'It's hormones,' he said. 'You're the least wet person I know.'

'It's still really kind of you to do this for me.'

There was nothing kind about it; she was expecting his baby and he wanted to take care of her. And what he was about to suggest didn't necessarily mean getting close to her; it just meant he was stepping up to his responsibility to her and to the baby. 'Maybe I can do this for a while,' he said, 'so you don't have to cook until you're feeling less tired.'

She blinked. 'You'd seriously come here every night just to cook me dinner?'

'Or we could alternate dinner between your place and

mine, but I'll do the cooking. If you come to me then you take a taxi, and I'll drive you home afterwards.'

She frowned. 'I can drive myself.'

He shook his head. 'I'd feel happier if you didn't.' As her frown deepened, he added, 'I'm not casting aspersions on your ability or anything like that. What I mean is that you're working full time and you're pregnant, tiredness is a symptom of early pregnancy and you need your rest, and driving in London isn't exactly restful.'

'There's the Tube. And walking. Walking's good for pregnant women. And I'll probably have to switch my dance aerobics class for an antenatal aqua aerobics class—given that I haven't quite rehabbed my foot yet,' she said with a grimace.

'Even so. I'd be happier if you let me drive you. Humour me?' he asked.

For a moment, he thought she was going to refuse; then she nodded. 'All right. And thanks. Actually, it'll be nice not to have to think about cooking. I'm not getting any morning sickness, but I'm just bone-deep tired. I really wasn't expecting to feel like this.'

'I wouldn't dare tell you to take it easy, especially as living with the walking cast drove you stir-crazy,' he said, 'but maybe you need to pace yourself a little bit until you get used to being pregnant. If I can take up the slack for you, I will. Whatever you need, just let me know.'

'OK. I appreciate it. Cooking dinner for me would be great,' she admitted. 'Just for a few days, until I get my energy back and stop falling asleep all the time.'

'It's going to be simple food,' he warned. 'You have no chance whatsoever of pomegranate molasses being one of the ingredients, but just tell me what you'd like or what you can't face eating, and I'll sort it out.'

She smiled. 'Probably not spicy food at the moment—I had the vegetable chilli yesterday for lunch at work and it gave me heartburn.'

'Noted.' He paused. 'Have you booked in to see your family doctor yet?'

'I've got an appointment at the end of the week, but you and I know the appointment's just routine and to get me logged into the system.'

'Are you going to book a dating scan?' he asked.

She winced. 'I kind of want to hold off until we know what's happening. I'll be ten weeks at the beginning of December, but we might not know your results by then—or, if we do and it's bad news, we'll need CVS to test the baby. So I'm going to try and stave it off for a couple of weeks more.'

The dating scan was the thing all his patients and their partners looked forward to most—actually seeing their baby on the screen. They all kept a copy of the scan photograph with them and showed it off proudly. Yet Dani couldn't relax and enjoy her pregnancy until she knew the truth about his DNA. This whole thing was a waiting game for both of them.

He wrapped his arms round her. 'Sorry. I feel as if I've taken all the joyful stuff out of pregnancy for you.'

'It's not your fault,' she said, though he knew she was being kind. Of course it was his fault. He was the one who might have the faulty gene.

'Do you want me to go with you when you have the counselling appointment?' she asked.

'No.' He could see the hurt in her expression, but what choice did he have? Until he knew whether he'd inherited Huntington's from Stephen, he needed to keep her at a distance. 'This is something I need to do by myself,' he said gently, 'but you have my full support and I'll be there for you and the baby. Anything you need, I'll be there.'

'The same goes for you.'

No, it didn't, but he wasn't going to get into a fight with her about it. 'Sit down and put your feet up, and I'll sort out dinner.'

'Thank you.'

She was almost asleep again in the fifteen minutes it took him to heat the bread through, heat the sauce, boil the kettle and cook the ravioli. And how he would've liked to curl up with her on the sofa with a good book, letting her use him as a pillow while she slept and holding her close, enjoying her warmth against him. But he couldn't allow himself that kind of domestic pleasure just yet. Maybe not ever, if his results said the wrong thing.

If only his mum had never met Stephen...

'Hey, sleepyhead.' He stroked her cheek. 'Dinner's ready.'

She blinked at him. And how he wanted to scoop her up and carry her to bed. Just to hold her. Be close to her.

Which was dangerous. He needed to keep that little bit of distance, for his sanity's sake.

'I laid the table in the kitchen,' he said. 'I hope you don't mind me rummaging around.'

'No, it's fine,' she said. 'Thank you.'

She was quiet throughout dinner, but he put that down to tiredness.

'Do you want me to run you a bath before I go?' he asked.

'No, because I'd probably fall asleep in it,' she said.

Just for a second, he could see wistfulness in her face. As if she'd wanted to ask him to stay and hold her until she slept. Something that any normal man would do for his pregnant partner.

But their situation wasn't normal. And he dared not let himself get close to her, in case the test showed the worst-case scenario. He absolutely wouldn't burden her, the way Stephen had burdened his partner.

'I'll see you tomorrow, then,' he said. 'Sleep well.'

She nodded. 'And thanks, Alex.'

Alex was relieved to have a call from his family doctor's surgery the next day, saying they had managed to fast-track an appointment for him and the counsellor could see him on Friday afternoon. Dani was already in clinic, and he could hardly interrupt her for something personal. Plus his own clinic was due to start in a couple of minutes.

In the end he texted her.

Counselling appointment Friday afternoon.

She'd pick it up later when she had time.

Then he looked at his first set of notes.

How ironic that today his first parents had a genetic problem in their family, though it was a haemoglobin problem rather than Huntington's. And they'd just had their CVS test results back.

This could so easily be Dani and himself, in a few weeks' time...

He pulled himself together and called the Giorgious in.

'Nice to meet you. I'm Alex Morgan,' he said. 'So how are you feeling, Mrs Giorgiou?'

'A lot better now we have the test results back,' she said feelingly. 'The last few weeks have been horrible, having to wait and not knowing whether our baby was going to be all right or whether he—well, or she—was going to have thalassaemia. I had no idea I was a haemoglobin Lepore carrier. Nobody in my family has ever had any symptoms and I only found out because of the routine antenatal testing.'

'That's when they called me in for screening,' Mr Giorgiou said. 'I was adopted, so I don't really have any medical history about my birth family. They did the tests and discovered I'm a carrier for beta thalassaemia.'

Alex knew that the beta thalassaemia and haemoglobin Lepore genes were more common in people with Southern European origins, like the Giorgious, but unless you had a family history you'd never suspect it. 'It must have been a bit of a shock to both of you,' he said.

'It was,' Mr Giorgiou agreed. 'I'd never even heard of thalassaemia or Lepore haemoglobin before, so I didn't have a clue how serious it was, or if it meant the baby would be ill or I'd be ill when I'm older.'

'The counsellor was really nice,' Mrs Giorgiou said. 'She explained that the baby would inherit one of two haemoglobin genes from each of us, either a normal one or a problem one. She drew us a diagram to show there was a one in two chance the baby was a carrier, a one in four chance the baby would be completely OK, and a one in four chance the baby would have inherited the problem gene from each of us and have full-blown thalassaemia.'

'She said if it was the worst-case scenario, the baby's blood cells would break down easily and he'd need a blood transfusion every three weeks, and medication for the rest of his life,' Mr Giorgiou said. 'I was horrified to think that we both feel so well, and yet we could've given our baby such a terrible disease. I looked it up on the Internet, and it looks as if the only cure is a bone marrow or stem cell transplant—and that's if you can find a suitable donor.'

'And there are risks from the transplant, too,' Mrs Giorgiou added. 'Waiting for the results was the worst two weeks of our lives.'

He could imagine it. Especially as he and Dani were just about to go through something similar. 'I'm very pleased to see from your notes that it wasn't the worst case,' Alex said.

'All the same,' Mrs Giorgiou said, 'I feel bad that the baby's a carrier. If his partner is as well, that means our grandchildren have a huge risk of getting thalassaemia.'

'Did the counsellor explain about PGD if you want to have another baby in the future?' Alex asked. 'She might have called it pre-implantation genetic diagnosis.'

Mr Giorgiou nodded. 'She said we could have IVF treatment and they could test the embryo to make sure the baby hadn't inherited the bad gene from either of us.'

'That's really good to know,' Mrs Giorgiou said. 'Because we do want more children, but we don't want to take the risk of the baby having full-blown thalassaemia. It's a one in four chance, and that's too high.'

The same risk that his and Dani's baby had of inheriting Huntington's. 'Of course.' Alex smiled at them. 'I've got the results through of the tests that the midwife did when you came in this morning, and I'm pleased to see that your urine sample's clear of any problems, your weight gain is average, and your blood pressure's fine. I'll just examine you now, if I may.'

The examination turned out to be perfectly routine. 'All's going well,' Alex said. 'Do you have any questions for me, or is there anything you're worrying about?'

'No—now we've got the results, it's all good,' Mrs Giorgiou said.

'The community midwife will see you for the triple test,' he said, 'and then it'll be your twenty-week scan here at Muswell Hill. If you're worried about anything in the meantime, talk to your midwife—she'll get in touch with us if she needs to.'

'Thank you.' The Giorgious shook his hand and left.

Alex wrote up his notes and stared thoughtfully at the screen. Would he and Dani be lucky enough to have good news? Or were they in for at least six weeks of waiting and worrying?

The rest of the week went quickly, and finally it was time for Alex's counselling appointment.

'Dr Morgan?' the counsellor said, coming into the waiting room.

He stood up. 'Call me Alex,' he said.

'And I'm Libby,' she said. 'Come through to my office. Can I get you a glass of water or a cup of tea?'

He shook his head. 'Thanks, but I'm fine.' He just wanted to get this over with.

'Your family doctor has told me the situation,' Libby said. 'We usually allow a month or so between appointments, so you've got time to think about things and process all the information.'

'I'm sorry, but I really don't have time for that,' Alex said. 'I asked my family doctor if we could fast-track it so we cover the first three appointments today.'

'In the circumstances, I completely understand why. You're a doctor, so I'm sure you already know most of the clinical stuff, but I still need to go through it with you,' she explained, 'because there's a huge difference between knowing something with your head and knowing it with your heart.'

He smiled wryly. 'That sounds like the kind of thing I say to my patients who have major complications—but nothing we say will change the result here. There's a baby involved, so for everyone's sake I need to know if I have the faulty gene or not. If I do, then we need prenatal testing, whereas if I don't my...' Dani wasn't his partner, but what else could he call her? 'My partner won't have to go through CVS.'

Chorionic villus sampling was where a tiny piece of the placenta was removed via a needle through the mother's abdomen; there was a small risk of miscarriage, and it also meant another three-week wait for the test results.

'I understand that the baby's your first concern,' Libby said, 'but you need to be prepared to face the implications for you, too—and your plans for the future might be affected by the test results.'

'I'm prepared to face it now,' Alex said. 'I admit I dragged my feet on this when it was just me affected by it, because I felt it was pointless knowing. If the test result is positive, there's nothing I can do to prevent getting Huntington's or even delay it. So it would just make my mum blame herself even more for the fact I have an incurable neurodegenerative disease.'

'Whereas right now it's an axe hanging over your head and you're going to wonder if every time you trip over or spill a cup of coffee or forget a word or get snappy with someone, it's the first sign of the disease,' Libby pointed out gently.

'There is that,' he said, 'but I'd rather have a good quality of life without knowing I'm definitely going to end up with it.' Even if it did mean keeping himself cut off from everyone.

'Most of people I see decide to take the test because they want to take out the uncertainty and plan for their future,' she said. 'The third most common reason is family planning.' She paused. 'Would it be useful for your partner to talk to me?'

'She's an obstetrician, too—she knows the procedures and the risks,' Alex said.

'So if your test is positive, you'll have prenatal testing?'

'That's why I need the test fast-tracked,' Alex said. 'Prenatal testing is usually done somewhere between eleven and fifteen weeks.'

'And your partner's how pregnant at the moment?'

'About seven weeks. It's still early days. But I know it takes time for you to get the test results, and if we need prenatal testing that'll be another three weeks, so I can't just wait until Dani's past the first trimester.'

'And you know that if you have prenatal testing, you'll have to agree to a termination if the baby's positive, because the baby can't give their consent?' Libby asked.

'Yes. And we'll deal with that when we come to it,' he said.

'If your result is positive,' she said, 'then you obviously know that for future family planning you can have pre-implantation—'

'—genetic diagnosis,' he finished with a smile. 'Yes. We can have IVF and the embryos will be tested, and we can use an embryo that hasn't inherited the mutated gene on chromosome four.'

She smiled back. 'I don't mean to sound patronising, Alex. Most of the people I see have done their research already, and you'll know more than average because of your job, but I still need to be sure that you know all your options and you've had a chance to think about what everything means.'

'I have,' he said, 'and I'm ready to sign a consent form saying that it's an informed decision.'

'Let's do the form first, then,' she said, and handed it to him. 'Read it through, and if you have any questions I'll do my best to answer them before you sign.'

He read it through. 'No questions,' he said, and signed it.

'Thank you. I'm going to take a blood sample for the test now. You already know that genes are made from DNA, and DNA is made from four chemicals—adenine, guanine, cytosine and thymine, all known by their initial letters. One section of the Huntington gene has three chemicals—CAG—repeated a number of times, and in the pre-symptomatic diagnosis test we look at the number of the CAG repeats on the gene.'

Alex already knew all this, but he wasn't going to push the issue; as Libby had told him, it was her job to be sure that he knew all the information and all the options.

'If there are about twenty-six repeats, that's normal; twenty-seven to thirty-five means it's an intermediate case and you probably won't develop the symptoms but you might still pass it on to your children; thirty-six to thirty-nine means it's an abnormal result and you might or might not get symptoms, most likely later in life; anything over forty means it's abnormal. I'm afraid that if you do have an abnormal result, we can't actually tell you when you'll start to develop symptoms, just that you will.'

'And a very large number of repeats makes the Huntingtin protein on the Huntington gene sticky and causes aggregates in the brain cells, which is what we think causes the cells to die off,' he said.

'You've clearly done your research,' she said. 'There are some studies going on looking at cell replacement therapies, and others looking at gene variants so we can look at biological pathways we should use to target new drug therapies, could be that we can repair damaged DNA.'

'But it's all in the early stages and there are no guarantees any of them will work,' he said.

'Everything has to start somewhere.' She took the blood sample and labelled it. 'I'll be in touch in two or three weeks, when we have the results back.'

'You can't just tell me over the phone?'

'No, I really can't,' she said gently. 'You've already bent the rules quite a bit—most of my patients have three appointments, with a gap in between them so they have a chance to get their heads round all the information.'

'Sorry.' He sucked in a breath. 'I know I'm being pushy. It's just…'

'Horrible having to wait,' Libby finished. 'All I can suggest is that you try to find some way of distracting yourself so you don't focus on the worst-case scenarios.'

'And try not to look things up on the Internet, because it's usually the extreme cases that come up first in a search engine,' he said. 'I say that to my patients all the time. I think I've got a lot more understanding about how they feel now.'

'I can't make you any promises,' Libby said. 'But when we do get the results back, I'll call you immediately.'

'Thank you.' He shook her hand. 'And I'm sorry that I'm a walking cliché.'

'You mean, medics always make the worst patients?'

she asked with a smile. 'I'll let you off. Try to have a good weekend. And if you do want to talk to me before the results come back, you've got my contact details.'

'Thanks. I appreciate it.' He shook her hand, then left the office and texted Dani.

Appointment went fine. Waiting game now.

She called him straight back. 'Are you OK?' she asked.

'I'm fine.' He lied automatically, not wanting to burden her. Right at that moment he didn't have a clue how he felt. Just numb.

'Stop pushing me away,' she said. 'We're in this together.'

No, they weren't. He'd seen the burden that Stephen's partner had carried, and he'd promised himself that he would never, ever put anyone in that situation. 'I'm fine.'

'If this baby is a boy,' she said, 'I sincerely hope he hasn't inherited your stubbornness, or the terrible twos is going to be the worst time of both our lives put together and quadrupled.'

And then it really hit him.

There was a one in four chance the baby might have Huntington's; but there was also a three in four chance the baby didn't have Huntington's. Which meant that next summer he'd be a dad.

A baby of his own.

It was something he'd always assumed would happen eventually, that he'd settle down with someone and raise a child. He'd planned to do that with Lara, until his mother had dropped the bombshell that Will wasn't his father and he might have inherited an incurable neurodegenerative condition. And since then his life had been stuck on hold.

'Alex? Are you still there?'

'Yes. Sorry.'

'You mean, your head's all over the place and you're thinking about the worst-case scenarios. When are the results back?'

'Two or three weeks.'

'So we're going to keep ourselves too busy to think. Days are easy because work's always busy,' she said. 'But evenings... Start making a list, Dr Morgan, of everything you've ever wanted to do in London. Because we're going to do the lot.'

'You need to pace yourself,' he reminded her.

'There is that. I might fall asleep on you—so you can drive,' she said. 'That way you'll still have to concentrate on something else if I'm zonked out. But in between we're going to keep too busy to think.'

Right at that moment he loved her for her bossiness.

And then he felt as if all the air had been sucked out of his lungs.

Loved?

He couldn't let himself think like that about Dani. Not until he knew the truth about his genetic history. And even then only if the results were the right ones.

'Alex. We'll start tonight,' she said. 'Dinner out. My shout. Come over right now.'

And even though he knew he ought to keep her at a distance, the warmth in her voice and the way she understood what was going on his head just drew him.

'I'm on my way.'

CHAPTER EIGHT

DANI LOOKED AT Alex narrowly when she opened the door to him, and he could practically feel the concern radiating from her.

'I'm fine,' he lied, before she could ask him.

'Like hell you are. You've just set a clock ticking. Nobody feels all right in those circumstances. Come here.' She hugged him.

He closed his eyes and rested his cheek against her hair. It would be so, so easy to kiss her, to lose himself in her. But that wouldn't be fair to either of them.

'Thank you for the hug,' he said, and pulled away.

There was a flash of hurt on her face, quickly masked, as if she realised that he was putting distance between them and hated it, but she understood his reasons.

'OK. Dinner. I managed to book us a table for seven o'clock,' she said, and I thought we'd take a stroll into the centre of Muswell Hill—because walking is good exercise for pregnant women and it's a good way to rehab my foot.'

It was overcast but not raining, so he didn't argue; he waited for her to put on her coat and then walked into the town centre with her. Every so often his hand accidentally brushed against hers, and he longed to catch her fingers between his and hold her hand properly. But how could he lead her on, with this axe hanging over their heads?

Her road was filled with beautiful Edwardian houses, some of which had clearly been turned into flats. Even though it was barely the second week of November, some people already had Christmas lights up outside their houses, varying from a simple string of fairy lights woven through the branches of a tree through to more elaborate displays, and most of the shops had displays of Christmas presents in their windows.

Dani had booked a quiet table in an Italian restaurant just off the Main Street. It was unlikely that anyone would see them together, but if they did no doubt Dani would claim it was a discussion about the ward's Christmas party. And Dani, he was beginning to realise, could be very persuasive. Left to his own devices, he would've sat on his own in his flat and brooded. She'd made him go out; even though some of the Christmassy music playing grated on him because it felt way too early—and this might turn out to be the worst Christmas of his life, so he really didn't want to think about it—at the same time the familiar music felt weirdly comforting.

Or maybe just being with Dani was comforting.

She chose chicken cacciatore with a side of mashed potatoes and buttered spinach; Alex ordered the same because he couldn't focus for long enough to concentrate on the menu, plus he didn't think he'd actually be able to taste anything.

She grabbed her phone. 'Right. Let's start making the Keeping Ourselves Too Busy To Think list.'

'Is this an extension of your Year of Saying Yes?' he asked. The Year of Saying Yes—which had got them into trouble in the first place.

'Sort of,' she said. 'We're going to make a list of things we'd like to do.'

'I can't actually think of anything,' he admitted. His head was full, but with the wrong stuff. All the what-ifs. Now he'd actually set the test process in motion, he couldn't stay in denial about his potential future.

Her eyes were filled with sympathy rather than pity, as if she knew exactly how he was feeling. 'OK, I'll start. We could go ice skating.'

'Apart from the fact that you're pregnant and it's not just you that might be hurt if someone knocks you over on the ice, you're still recovering from a fractured meta-tarsal,' he reminded her. 'Is ice skating really going to be the best thing for your foot?'

'Maybe not.' She gave him a grin. 'So I guess bungee jumping is out of the question, then?'

'Of course it—' He stopped as the penny dropped. 'Oh. You were teasing.'

'Not about the ice skating,' she said. 'I love the whole kit and caboodle, all the music and the lights and the skating and the hot chocolate, but the Christmas rinks won't be open for at least another week anyway. Though that means my foot will have another week's rehab before they open.'

'That's still a no to skating,' he said.

'Are you telling me that you can't skate, Dr Morgan? Tsk.' She pursed her lips. 'You know, I could teach you.'

'Not this year.'

'OK.' She sighed. 'So you're saying we can't do anything physical.'

Nothing that would put them up close and really personal. Dancing was completely out of the question. Not that he had the words to tell her that. 'We could do ten-

pin bowling,' he said, seizing on what she'd organised
for the ward's last team night out and which he'd managed to avoid.

'All right. I'll add that to the list. And we could go to
some shows—comedy or music,' she suggested.

'I'm not a huge fan of opera,' he said, 'but I'd be up
for anything else.'

'I'm not an opera fan either. We'll add a couple of
shows. How about museums?'

'I've already visited the main ones a few times over
the years,' he said, 'but I guess they're so big that you
can always find something new at every visit.'

'Or we could go to some of the lesser-known museums,' she said. She tapped something into a search engine and scrolled down the list of results. 'Here's one I've
definitely never been to. Apsley House—it was Welling-
ton's home, so you get the military history you used to
share with your granddad and I get the social history I
shared with my mum.'

He was surprised that she'd remembered what he'd
told her about his grandfather; then again, at work he
knew she paid attention to detail.

'Apparently the house has fabulous artwork,' she said.
'It's only open at weekends at this time of year, though.'

'We ought to make a note of opening times anyway,'
he said.

'Agreed. And maybe we can do some of the touristy
things we haven't got round to doing,' she said. 'How
about the London Eye?'

'And the Cutty Sark,' he said.

'Madame Tussaud's?'

Between them they managed to come up with a list
by the time the waiter brought their meal.

'So what we'll do when we get back to my place,' she said, 'is write each idea separately on a slip of paper, stick them in a jar and shake them up, and we take out a piece of paper every evening—that's what we'll do the next evening, or if it's something where we can't get tickets we'll book that for another time and take out a new bit of paper for something to plan the next night's distraction.'

'I can see why they get you to organise most of the ward's social stuff,' he said wryly.

She spread her hands and grinned. 'Because I'm horrendously bossy?'

'Because,' he said, 'you're full of great ideas. And I really appreciate you doing this for me, Dani. Waiting is... Well, I had patients earlier this week who'd had to wait for the results of genetic testing after CVS, after she found out at routine screening that she was a haemoglobin Lepore carrier; when they tested the dad, they discovered he was a beta thalassaemia carrier.'

Dani frowned. 'That's a tricky combination. Is the baby OK?'

'The baby's a carrier, but at least it's not going to have full-blown thalassaemia,' he said. 'They were lucky.'

'Hopefully we'll be lucky, too.'

But was hope enough?

Back at her flat, they went through the list of suggestions and wrote each one down on a piece of paper, then folded the piece of paper and dropped it into a jar.

'You pick tomorrow's,' Dani said.

He placed his hand over the top of the jar, gave it a shake, drew out a slip and read it out. '"The British Museum".'

'Which is one of my favourite places in the world,'

she said with a smile. 'Meet you at the Tube station to-morrow at half-past eight and we'll head off to Holborn?'

'Are you sure that's not too early? You look a bit tired,' he said.

'I'm fine.'

He gave her a speaking look. 'Now who's fibbing?'

'I'll be fine.' She paused. 'Alex, do you want to stay here tonight?'

He stared at her, not sure what to say. Part of him wanted to be with her; part of him knew he needed to keep his distance. And he hated being torn apart like this.

She sighed. 'I'm not propositioning you, if that's what you're thinking. And anyway, considering we've already... Well.' She rested her hand on her abdomen. 'What I meant was if you'd rather not be on your own, you're very welcome to stay. It's possible for us to share a bed without having sex.'

That was the real problem. The intimacy. Getting close to her, getting used to waking up with her in his arms—it would be oh, so easy. Dani's warmth and energy drew him like a magnet. But what if his test was positive? It would make things so much harder if he'd got close to her by then and had to back away. Better to keep his distance now.

'I'll be fine,' he lied.

'More like you'll be lying awake at stupid o'clock with all the worst-case scenarios running through your head,' she said.

How well she knew him. Or maybe it was what any normal person would do in his situation. He had no idea. But he definitely couldn't let himself give in to the longing to stay with her. Not tonight. Not until he knew where he stood, in genetic terms. 'I'm going to walk home,' he said, 'and by the time I get home I'll be physically tired and I'll sleep.'

'But if you can't, ring me,' she said.

Of course he wasn't going to be selfish enough to do that. He'd sit and flick through channels on the television and find something to distract him until his eyes closed. 'You need your sleep,' he reminded her.

'But I can still be there for you.' And her smile made his heart skip a bit. 'Just, if I fall asleep on your shoulder on the Tube tomorrow and start snoring, I'll need to you to sing or something to drown me out so people don't laugh at me.'

He couldn't help smiling. 'OK. See you tomorrow. And thank you.'

When Dani joined Hayley at the table in the canteen, she thought her best friend looked terrible, as if she wasn't sleeping. She'd seen Hayley this unhappy before, and reached over to squeeze her hand. 'Are you OK?'

'Yes—well, trying,' Hayley admitted.

'You're still worrying over your daredevil doctor?' Dani asked wryly.

'One who jumped into the canal the other day, to rescue a small child.'

'To be fair, that's a good thing to do,' Dani pointed out.

'I know. Which is why I hate myself for overreacting. We had a huge row about it and I'm still feeling guilty. He's a good man, Dani.'

'And you love him.' Dani tried not to think about her own feelings for Alex. Or her growing conviction that he wouldn't be able to love her back.

'It's complicated,' Hayley said.

'But worth fighting for,' Dani said. 'I like him. A lot. He's good for you—and I think you're good for him.'

'Yeah.' Hayley wrinkled her nose. 'I just need to learn to stop worrying.'

'Something like that,' Dani agreed.

'At least we've got dance aerobics class tonight. That always makes me feel better,' Hayley said.

'Ah. I'm not going to be able to make it for a couple of weeks.'

'Oh, no—I hope you haven't fractured your foot again.' Hayley looked concerned. 'Have you been running on it?'

'No and no,' Dani reassured her. 'I'm being sensible. No, just a friend is having a bit of a rough time and I'm trying to distract them.'

'Right. Well, if you need a co-distractee…'

Trust Hayley to offer. 'Thanks, Haze. I'll let you know,' Dani said. 'Oh, and Alex from my department is joining us for lunch when his clinic finishes.'

'Alex.' Hayley raised an eyebrow. 'Is there anything you want to tell me?'

Tons. But she thought that Hayley had enough to worry about. 'Just helping him settle into the department and get to know people better. You know what a bossy, interfering cow I am.'

'What a lovely, organised woman with a huge heart you are,' Hayley corrected. 'I could smack Leo. How did he manage to convince you that it was all your fault when he's such a cheating, lying slimeball?' She reached over the table and hugged Dani. 'You deserve so much better than him, Dani.'

'Uh-huh.' And even though Dani knew Leo had lashed out to try and distract himself from his own guilty feelings, she still wondered if there was a lot of truth in what he'd said. That she'd never find someone to love her because she was unloveable.

'You *do*.' Hayley stuck her hand up and waved. 'Alex,' she explained at Dani's mystified look. 'Let's change the subject.'

'Good idea,' Dani agreed.

Having lunch with Dani and Hayley made Alex realise what a hole there was in his own life. Seeing them together, the way they were so in tune, made him miss his own best friend. Especially as Tom had been the first friend he'd made at university.

Maybe he needed to start rebuilding some bridges.

He called Tom that evening on the way to Dani's from the supermarket—they'd agreed to chill out with a film in her living room rather than going out, as Dani had actually admitted to being tired. His heart was thumping madly; would Tom even speak to him, or would he just refuse to answer the call? Had he changed his number?

If the call went to voicemail, he'd hang up.

But then he heard Tom's voice, so familiar and yet sounding strange at the same time. 'Hey, Alex. How are you?'

So simple. So accepting. Why wasn't Tom giving him a hard time for spending the last ten months resolutely out of contact? 'I'm getting there,' he said carefully.

'Your head's in a better place now?' Tom asked.

Alex frowned. 'How much do you know?'

'When you did your big burning of bridges thing and sent me that text saying you'd gone travelling and you might not be back for a year, I rang your dad, because I thought you might be having some kind of breakdown and we needed to do an intervention,' Tom said. 'And he told me everything.'

'Oh.' Yet Will had said nothing to Alex. 'So you know about Stephen.'

'And the Huntington's. And the fact you don't want to take the test. Yes. You *idiot*. None of that was a valid reason for pushing all your friends away.' But it was said with affection. 'Did travelling help?'

'Not that much,' Alex admitted. 'And I'm sorry. You're right. I shouldn't have pushed anyone away, and you're the one person I probably should've talked to about it. But I had a hard job getting my head round it, and when I actually met Stephen...' He sighed. 'I guess it freaked me, seeing what the worst-case scenario looked like. And I just didn't want to be a burden to anyone, the way he was.'

'Idiot,' Tom said again. 'Of course you'd never be a burden. That's not how friendship works. You're there for each other in the good times and the bad. And if you do end up needing full nursing care, you're going to be bored out of your skull and need to see a few different faces during your week, aren't you?'

'Um.' Alex squirmed. 'So you kept in touch with Dad?'

'Yes. He said you were working in Muswell Hill. I thought about ringing you and suggesting we go out for a pint, but I wasn't sure you were ready to talk to me. I've been kind of hoping you'd call me.'

'A pint,' Alex said, 'sounds really good. And I'm sorry. I've behaved really badly.'

'Yup,' Tom agreed. 'But I don't think any of us knows how we'd really react in your situation until it happens.' He paused. 'So when are you free for that pint?'

'It's a bit complicated at the moment,' Alex said. 'A couple of weeks?' And then, if the results went his way, maybe he could ask Tom how he felt about being his best man. And godfather to the baby.

Which was when he realised just how much he wanted that. A life with Dani and their baby. No shadows of an incurable disease hanging over them.

'OK. Call me when you're ready.'

'Tom. Thanks. For not giving me the hard time I deserve.'

'Oh, I have years and years to make you suffer,' Tom said.

Alex could practically see the mischievous grin on his best friend's face. 'For what it's worth, I've missed you.'

'And I missed you, too, mate. Welcome back.'

'Thanks. I'd better go. Talk to you soon.'

'"Soon" had better be less than ten months this time,' Tom said.

'It will be. I promise.' His heart lighter, Alex ended the call.

Over the next couple of weeks, Alex and Dani were both busy at work. Christmas cards started to appear on all the noticeboards along with the thank-you cards from grateful new parents, and the reception area was decorated with a tree, tinsel and baubles. But Dani didn't think it felt quite like Christmas for either of them. She was remembering the run-up to Christmas last year, when Leo had made his shock announcement; and Alex was growing more and more tense with each day that passed, bringing his test results closer.

There was nothing either of them could do to influence the results of the test. Either he had the faulty gene or he didn't. But she kept him busy with their jar of distractions, and he was careful to make sure she didn't tire herself out.

But the hardest thing for Dani was the fact Alex was resolutely stubborn about keeping his distance. She knew he worried about being a burden, but couldn't he see that it didn't have to be that way? And if he did have the faulty gene, surely now—when he didn't have any symptoms— was the time to live life to the full?

Or was she just kidding herself, thinking that he was keeping his distance until he knew the results of the test, when in reality he just wasn't interested in a real relationship with her and she was expecting more than he was prepared to give?

The stupid thing was, the more time she spent with him, the more she grew to like him.

She more than liked him. Being with him made the world seem a brighter place, and she enjoyed sharing discoveries with him at museums on their dates-that-weren't-really-dates.

Which was really dangerous. Hadn't she learned her lesson from Leo—that it was pointless trying to love someone who didn't love you back?

Dani was still brooding about it when Hayley met her for lunch in the last week of November.

'I have some news,' Hayley announced.

'You've been promoted?' Dani guessed.

'Better than that.' She leaned forward. 'Sam asked me to marry him, last night. And I said yes.'

'That's fantastic!' Dani reached across the table and hugged her. 'I'm so pleased for you.'

'And I really want you to be my bridesmaid,' Hayley said. 'If you'd like to.'

'Like to? I'd be thrilled. That's just wonderful.' Dani grinned at her. 'It's the best news I've heard in ages.'

'And you'll help me choose a dress?'

'Of course I will. When do you want to go shopping?'

'As soon as possible,' Hayley said.

Dani blinked. 'When's the wedding?'

Hayley looked awkward. 'That's the thing—it's Christmas Eve.'

'*This* Christmas Eve? As in about a month away?' Dani asked.

'Um, yes.' Hayley bit her lip. 'Sam and I got a bit carried away with not wanting to wait any longer than we have to to get married, and a Christmas wedding would be so romantic—but I know what Christmas Eve means to you.'

The day Dani's husband had walked out on their marriage, saying there was someone else and they were expecting a baby. And Dani hadn't been looking forward to the first anniversary.

But no way was she going to rain on Hayley's parade. 'Actually,' Dani said, 'I'm really glad you're getting married on Christmas Eve. Because it means that this year I'm going to have a really, really good day on Christmas Eve. As your bridesmaid, I get to wear a gorgeous dress; I get to eat good food; and I get to have a good old dance with my mates—that is, I assume there's going to be dancing at your reception?'

'There certainly is—we're going to ask Maybe Baby to play, if they can make it.' Hayley looked anxious. 'But are you sure you don't mind the date? Because we can change it.'

'I'm really sure,' Dani said. 'Don't change it. I'm thrilled for both of you. This year, I'm going to have a happy Christmas Eve.' She pushed away the thought that Alex's test could be positive and if that happened then they'd be waiting for the results of their baby's screening test. 'And I'm going to be having too much fun to think about what it was like last year.' Her smile faded. 'There is one thing, though. Being Christmas, they're bound to play certain songs—is there any chance you can ask Maybe Baby not to play "Last Christmas"? Just I don't quite think I can handle the lyrics this year.'

'Of course I will.'

'It's going to be a while yet before I stop myself skipping it on the Christmas anthologies,' Dani said. 'We've got the ward's Christmas party next week, and I've asked Anton if he can keep it off the set list.'

Hayley gave her a hug. 'We're going to have only happy Christmas songs at the reception. Stuff like "All I Want For Christmas Is You".'

'Brilliant. Have you actually sorted out an "our song"?'

'Three of them,' Hayley said with a broad smile. 'Bach's "Air on a G String" while I walk down the aisle.'

'That's nice.'

Her smile broadened. 'Then "All You Need Is Love" when we sign the register.'

Dani laughed. 'I *so* know where you've pinched that from—and we are going to get the chance to watch our favourite Christmas movie together in December, aren't we?'

'We certainly are,' Hayley said. 'I'm not missing the Christmas Lobster for anything. And then we're having Bruno Mars' "Just The Way You Are" for the first dance.'

'I like that,' Dani said. 'Because it sounds as if you've come to terms with Sam being Sam.'

'Doing all his dangerous stuff,' Hayley said, but Dani could tell the grumpiness was feigned.

Dani smiled. 'It's the Year of Saying Yes, remember.'

'Not that you seem to have been doing too much of that yourself, Dani,' Hayley pointed out.

Oh, but she had. Which was why she was nine weeks pregnant right now. Part of her longed to confide in her best friend—but if she told Hayley that she was pregnant, then she'd have to tell her the rest of it. That Alex was taking responsibility for the baby and looking after her, and they were sort of dating each other to keep their minds off things—but they also weren't quite dating because he was keeping his distance, either because he was scared about being a burden to her or because he didn't love her but didn't want to let her down. And that she and Alex might have a really hideous decision to make, if his test results came back positive. The whole thing was such a mess, and she didn't want to drag Hayley into the middle of it. Especially now, when Hayley was planning to marry the man she loved and who loved her all the way back.

Instead, she smiled sweetly. 'Maybe I'll meet someone at your wedding reception.'

'You have to say yes to everyone who asks you to dance, you know,' Hayley warned.

Dani smiled. 'Of course. So is your engagement common knowledge, or is it still under wraps?'

'It's still under wraps. You're the only person we've told apart from our parents,' Hayley said, 'but Sam's going to propose to me at the ward's Christmas party—it'll be the last gift in the Secret Santa.'

'That's so romantic. So when do you want me to go dress shopping with you?'

'This weekend?'

'Sure.' Dani felt slightly guilty, as it meant Alex would have some time alone when he wouldn't be distracted and could brood about things, but she would still be able to see him in the evening.

Part of her was tempted to ask Hayley if she could bring a plus one to the wedding, but then again everything was still up in the air. The results of Alex's Huntington's test were due any time in the next week, and if they were positive then the last thing he'd want to do was to go to a wedding. Plus, if his results were positive then she would've had the CVS and be waiting for the results of that, too.

She pushed the thought aside. 'What else can I do to help?' she asked.

'I've done a Dani and made a list of things to tick off,' Hayley said with a grin, 'and I think we're pretty much sorted. Sam's arranging everything at the register office and the venue, so the major thing left is the dress.'

'Unless you know someone who can make it for you and actually has space in their schedule, we're going to have to look at dresses you can buy off the peg, because there won't be time to have it made for you,' Dani said, remembering her own wedding and the time it had taken to have the dresses made to measure.

'Maybe we can sit down with my laptop tomorrow night and make a shortlist of dresses we like and which shops they're in,' Hayley said, 'and then I can check if the shop has the dresses in the right size for us to try on Saturday.'

'Perfect plan,' Dani said with a smile.

* * *

That evening, Dani went to the cinema with Alex, and was mortified to find that she'd nodded off in the middle of the film.

'Was I snoring?' she asked, squirming.

'Yes, but fortunately it was an action film and the explosions on screen were louder than your snores. Just.'

'Very funny.' She paused. 'Alex, there's something I need to talk to you about. I'm so sorry to let you down, but I can't do our distraction thing tomorrow night. I know you'll keep this confidential—Hayley's getting married on Christmas Eve, and I need to help her with her wedding dress. She asked me to go over to her place tomorrow and help her with a shortlist, and then on Saturday we're going to try them on. I'll be as fast as I can.'

'Take as long as you need,' he said. 'In the circumstances, Hayley's wedding should take precedence.'

'I want to support both of you. Maybe we can do something in the evening?' Dani suggested.

'Sure.' He paused. 'Does Hayley know?'

'About what?'

'The baby.' He dragged in a breath. 'My test.'

'No, to both.'

'So I'm your only support, too.' He paused. 'You really ought to tell her.'

'I don't want to be a burden to her.' Dani shook her head. 'Not now, when she's got a chance to be really happy again. I think I told you, her fiancé Evan was killed in an industrial fire a year and a half ago, trying to save someone, and it broke her heart. Although she and Sam got close, he's on the MERIT team, which means he's putting himself at risk in the same way that Evan did, and she found it pretty hard to deal with the idea.'

'But obviously they've sorted it out now.' He looked at her. 'You've been nagging me when I say I don't want to be a burden to anyone, but you're doing exactly the same thing.'

'No, I'm not. I fully intend to tell her everything. Just not until after the wedding. I want her to enjoy her special day without worrying about me.'

'I guess.' He sighed. 'I'm sorry. I wish things were different.'

That he didn't have the spectre of Huntington's in his genetic make-up? Or that he was in love with her and they would make a life with the baby together?

She didn't dare ask—because she wasn't sure she could cope with the answer.

'And are you OK about the wedding being on Christmas Eve?' he asked, surprising her.

'Yes.'

'Really?' he checked. 'Because that's obviously something else you wouldn't be able to tell her.'

'Actually, she's already asked me the same question,' Dani said. 'And it is fine. Because at least this year I have my best friend's wedding to enjoy. I'm going to have a great Christmas Eve, with good food and good music and a pretty dress, instead of having the person I thought loved me stomping all over my heart. I'm looking forward to the wedding. Sam's a nice guy and he's going to make my best friend really happy. Which makes me really happy.'

'That's good.' He saw her back to her front door. 'Well. I'll see you at work tomorrow.'

'You're welcome to come in for a coffee or whatever.'

He shook his head. 'You need your sleep.'

It felt like an excuse. What had made him so antsy? she wondered. Was it the discussion about weddings? Or was he using this as an excuse to distance himself from her even more?

CHAPTER NINE

ALEX WAS SHOCKED to discover how much he missed Dani's company the following evening. And he felt at a total loss on Saturday. He spent the morning at the gym, then did his Christmas shopping in the afternoon—and he found himself having no idea what to do about Dani. Should he buy her a present? They weren't exactly dating, but she was expecting his baby, so she counted as more than just a colleague. Their whole relationship was back to front and upside down.

Once he got the test results, they could move on. But he was still waiting to hear, and every day that passed seemed to drag on for longer and longer and longer. Several times now he'd had to stop himself ringing Libby and asking her if something had gone wrong or if he'd missed a message. Given the time of year, there was a strong chance that someone in the lab or Libby herself had gone down with a virus, and that was the reason for the delay. Maybe there was a backlog in the lab. There was nothing he could do to influence things, so he'd just have to wait until they were ready to give him the results. But patience, he thought, was seriously overrated as a virtue.

Finally, on the day of the ward's Christmas party,

Libby left a message on his voicemail. 'Can you call the office to make an appointment, please?'

He went cold.

That had to mean the results were finally in.

Which meant that the axe was about to fall. Whether it was going to hit him or miss him, he had absolutely no idea. He had no control over this at all.

Oh, for pity's sake. Why couldn't Libby have told him in her message and put him out of his misery, instead of making it drag out like this?

His hand was actually shaking as he returned the call.

'It's Alex Morgan. Libby asked me to call to make an appointment,' he said when the receptionist answered.

'Of course,' the receptionist said. 'Would you like to come in today?'

Which meant even more waiting. Except now that there was a definite time limit to the wait, it was unbearable. 'Could you tell me the test result over the phone, please?'

'I'm sorry, I'm afraid I don't have access to the results.'

He dug his nails into his palm in sheer frustration. 'OK. Could Libby tell me?'

'She's with another patient right now, I'm afraid, so I can't put you through to her. We don't make appointments for Fridays, so shall I make you an appointment for next week if you can't make today?'

'I can make today,' Alex said quickly. If he had to keep waiting, he'd be a basket case by tomorrow, let alone next week. 'When can you fit me in?'

'Half-past five?'

It would mean he'd have to leave early, but he'd have a quiet word with the head of department to explain and he was pretty sure it wouldn't be a problem. 'That's fine,' he said. 'Thank you. I'll be there.'

Should he ask Dani to go with him? he wondered as he ended the call. Then again, it would be too complicated to get her to leave early, too, especially on the day of the ward's Christmas party when everyone would be going to the pub straight from work and she was the main organiser of the event. She already had enough on her plate. Plus, if it was bad news, he'd rather that she heard it from him once he'd had a chance to come to terms with it.

If it was bad news, then he'd send her a text saying that he'd gone down with a virus and was sorry to dump all the Christmas party stuff on her. And then he'd work out just how he was going to break the real news to her first thing tomorrow.

Somehow he managed to deal with a ward round, a clinic and an emergency Caesarean section. Dani was in clinic all day and he didn't get a chance to see her, let alone leave her a message. And what could he say, in any case? After a quiet explanation to their head of department, he left the ward and headed to Libby's office.

Her previous appointment was running fifteen minutes late. By the time the counsellor finally called him in, Alex felt sick with anxiety.

'Come in and sit down, Alex,' she said with a smile.

Was that a smile of relief, because it was good news; or a smile of sympathy, because it was bad news? He didn't have a clue. This was worse than waiting for all his exam results rolled into one—far worse, because at least with exams he'd had a good idea how he'd performed, but with this there was no way of knowing and it was completely out of his control.

'Your results are back,' she said, 'and I'm pleased to say there are twenty-five CAG repeats.'

He stared at her, trying to process what she'd just said. *Twenty-five CAG repeats.*

Finally it clicked. 'That's in the normal range. At the top end of the range, but still normal. So you're saying I don't have Huntington's?' he checked.

'You don't have Huntington's,' she confirmed.

He blew out a breath. 'You could've told me that in your message. Or your receptionist could have told me that over the phone.'

Libby shook her head. 'We've been through that, Alex. We always give the results face to face, never in a message or over the phone. And we never give results on a Friday because we don't want anyone being unsupported over a weekend. Having a negative result has just as much impact as a positive one.'

'Of course it doesn't—a positive result means the axe hanging over you actually falls on your neck, whereas a negative one means it misses,' he snapped. Then he grimaced. 'I'm sorry, Libby. That was unfair of me. I've been on tenterhooks waiting for the results, but that doesn't give me the right to take out my frustrations on you, and I apologise.'

'No problem. It's a perfectly normal reaction, and I'm not going to take it personally. As I was saying,' she said gently, 'having a negative result can have a huge impact on you. You've had your life on hold for months, and now you can move on again. Of course you're going to be relieved, but there are going to be all sorts of other emotions in there as well—guilt that you might have hurt someone over the situation, or made them worry about you. And this has been a real emotional ordeal for you, because you're not the only one affected by the result.'

He rubbed a hand over his eyes. 'This means the baby's OK. I don't have the bad gene, so I can't have passed it on. Dani won't have to have CVS, and we won't have to worry about making a really hideous decision.' He looked at Libby. 'Actually, I can't quite take this in.' He'd tried to prepare himself for the worst-case scenario, because the odds were so high. And now that worry wasn't there any more, he felt disorientated.

'Can I get you a glass of water or a cup of tea?' she asked.

He shook his head. 'Thanks, but I need to go. I'm supposed to be at the ward's Christmas party. I'm co-organising it.' Not that he'd done a huge amount. Dani had shouldered the burden.

'Can you text your co-organiser with a white lie and say you've got a tummy bug or something?'

He smiled wryly. 'That was my plan if the test was positive. But it's not. And now I can move on.'

'It might be an idea to have some time to yourself, just to process the news and get used to the idea,' Libby warned. 'Because sometimes relief puts people in a bit of a whirl, and they end up saying the wrong things.'

'No. I need to tell Dani.' And, more than that, now he knew he didn't have to keep himself at a distance any more, he could finally act on the feelings he had towards her. This would be a new beginning for Dani, himself and the baby. 'Thank you, Libby,' he said. He shook her hand. 'Thank you for everything.'

Once he'd left the building, he called his parents.

His mother answered. 'Alex? Is everything all right?'

'Everything's fine, Mum. I'm in a bit of a rush right

now as I'm on the way to the ward's Christmas party, but I wanted you to be the first to know. I took the test for Huntington's, and I'm fine. So you don't have to worry any more. It's all good.'

'Oh, Alex. Thank God you're all right. Thank God my stupidity…'

He could hear her crying, and guilt twisted into him. He should've done this when she'd first told him the news about Stephen, instead of leaving her to wait and worry and come to the worst conclusions. He'd thought he was being oh, so noble—but now he realised he'd actually been stubborn and unreasonable and selfish. And he felt thoroughly ashamed of himself. 'I'm sorry, Mum. For everything. But it's all going to be OK now.' He swallowed hard. 'I'll take you and Dad out to dinner next week to celebrate,' he said. 'We'll talk soon. I have to go. But I love you, Mum. And Dad. Tell him for me.'

'Love you, too,' she said through her tears.

At the pub, there simply wasn't time to tell Dani the news—there were last-minute things to sort out. Besides, he didn't want to tell her in front of a room full of people. He'd wait until the end of the evening, when he saw her home and it would be just the two of them.

He wasn't sitting anywhere near Dani during the meal; instead he was with Jas and Gilly, the midwives, but thanks to Dani making him go to lunch with them so he got to know them better, he was relaxed in their company and found himself enjoying the party and the banter. He felt slightly guilty that the box of posh chocolates he'd brought as a Secret Santa present was so boring, when so many of the others were inventive and clearly based on long-standing departmental jokes. But the food was good, the company was good, the jokes in the crackers were incredibly corny, and he liked the fact that even their head of department was wearing a paper hat and joining in with the raucousness.

And he didn't have to fake a single one of his smiles.

After the meal, Anton and Gilly left the table and joined the rest of the band on stage; once the tables had been cleared away, everyone started dancing and singing along to the Christmas favourites that the band were playing.

He didn't get a chance to see Dani until Maybe Baby started playing a slow dance. 'Dance with me?' he asked.

She smiled back at him. 'Sure.'

It felt so good to hold her close.

He desperately wanted to tell her the good news, but now really wasn't the right time—they needed to be on their own. But hopefully she'd let him see her home and he could tell her then.

At the end of the night, the staff who were on early shift the next morning had already gone home. The band packed up their gear, and everyone else said their goodbyes.

'Can I walk you home?' Alex asked.

'OK,' Dani said.

He smiled at her. 'It was a good night,' he said.

Yes, and it had been nice to see him come completely out of his shell and relax with everyone; she'd seen him laughing with Jas and Gilly at the far end of the table from her. She knew how tense he was about the results he was still waiting for, so she was glad that the party had been a kind of light relief for him.

But something was still bothering her. 'Where did you

disappear to before the party? I thought you might've been in Theatre, but someone said they'd seen you leave the ward earlier.'

'I had an appointment. The counsellor rang me,' he said.

She blinked at him. 'You mean you've got the results?'

'Yes. And I'm clear. Twenty-five CAG repeats. I don't have Stephen's faulty gene.'

She stopped dead, flung her arms round him and hugged him. 'You're all right. You're not going to get Huntington's!' She held him tighter. 'And that means the baby's OK, too.'

Everything was going to be all right. Especially as his arms were wrapped round her. Relief and joy flooded through her. They wouldn't have to make a hideous decision. It was going to be fine.

But then, as they stood there together, the little bubbles of joy started to burst as she realised the implications of what he'd just said. She pulled away and stared at him. 'Wait. You've known all night that you don't have the gene and you didn't tell me until now?'

'The middle of the ward's Christmas party is hardly the easiest place for a conversation—especially for one like this.'

'You could have texted me,' she pointed out.

'I wanted to tell you myself, not send you an impersonal text message as if it was something that didn't really matter.' He looked at her. 'I don't want to fight, Dani.'

'Neither do I.' But she was hurt, all the same. Something as important as this, and he hadn't included her. Even though they were in this together. If it had been the other way round, she would have made the time to tell him. How stupid she'd been to think that they'd got closer over the last few weeks. How stupid she'd been to let herself fall for another man who didn't love her back. 'You didn't even tell me you had the appointment.'

'I didn't get a chance. They called this morning. And you and I haven't exactly been in the same place all day. I wasn't just going to leave you a text so you worried yourself sick with waiting. Believe me,' he said, his voice dry, 'waiting for news when you know you won't hear for weeks is nothing like knowing you're actually going to hear in a few short hours. It's like all your exam results days rolled into one, except this time you haven't got a clue what the result's going to be.'

'You still could've told me.' But instead he'd chosen to block her out, yet again.

'I'm sorry.' He sighed. 'But we don't have to worry about the baby any more, Dani. Everything's going to be fine.'

And she didn't have to hold off on the scan. She could finally let herself think about the child growing inside her and make plans for their future. Part of her was thrilled, but part of her was hurt at the way he'd excluded her yet again. 'Uh-huh.'

'And we can get married.'

Had she just heard him correctly? 'What?'

'We can get married,' he repeated.

Marriage wasn't something they'd ever discussed. Alex had made it clear that he'd step up to his responsibilities for the baby, but he hadn't said anything about his relationship with her. They'd tacitly left it that he wasn't in a good place until he knew the truth about his genetic heritage; and they wouldn't discuss it until then. She'd thought maybe they'd got closer on their dates-that-weren't-really-dates, but he'd said nothing about his feelings.

And now he was casually saying that they could get married?

He wasn't telling her that he loved her and wanted to be with her, or making any kind of declaration of his feelings towards her at all. Just the plain, bald statement that they could get married. Almost as if he was suggesting a trip out or having fish for dinner on Friday instead of sharing his life with her.

So he wasn't asking her to marry him because he loved her. This had to be a mixture of guilt and responsibility talking; he was suggesting that they should get married simply because he thought he ought to, for the baby's sake.

No way.

Dani been married before, but Leo had at least loved her when they'd got married, even if he'd fallen out of love with her afterwards. And she knew what it felt like being married to someone who'd fallen out of love with her. How much worse would it be if she married someone who didn't love her in the first place?

'No,' she said.

He stared at her. 'What do you mean, no?'

'I mean,' she said, 'my best friend is about to get married to someone she loves deeply—someone who loves her all the way back. I'm not prepared to settle for less than that. So, no, Alex, I won't marry you.'

Why was he looking so shocked? Did he really think she'd marry him just to give the baby his name? This was the twenty-first century. They could sort out the baby's name and he could see the baby without them having to be married.

Alex had spent the last few months being stubborn about not letting people close because he'd thought he'd be a burden to them in the future—wrongly, on all counts. Well, now it was her turn to be stubborn. Though she was pretty sure her reasons were a great deal sounder than his had been. She absolutely wasn't going to get married to someone who didn't love her.

'Right now,' she said, 'I think you have an awful lot of bridges to rebuild. I suggest you go home and make a start on that.'

He lifted his chin. 'I said I'd see you home safely.'

'I'm thirty-two years old, and I'm perfectly capable of seeing myself home safely,' she said wearily. 'Right now, I don't even want to talk to you.' She wanted to push him in a puddle, but fortunately for him the evening was dry. 'Please, just go home.'

'Dani—'

'Go home, Alex,' she said, and turned away from him.

Alex stared at Dani as she walked away.

It was late, and she was pregnant. The decent thing to do would be to see her home safely, make sure that she was all right.

But she'd made it very clear she didn't want him to do that.

OK. He'd compromise and walk behind her at a suitable distance. Far enough away that he wasn't going to crowd her or upset her, but near enough to be at her side in a few seconds if he was needed.

Doggedly, he walked behind her, keeping a good thirty metres between them and hanging back at the corner of her road. As soon as she closed her front door behind her and he knew she was safe, he walked back to his own flat.

Why had she refused his proposal?

He thought about it.

'My best friend is about to get married to someone she loves deeply—someone who loves her all the way back. I'm not prepared to settle for less than that. So, no, Alex, I won't marry you.'

Was she saying she didn't love him?

Or was she saying she didn't think that he loved her?

He could ask her for clarification, but right now she'd made it clear she didn't want to talk to him. And he could hardly ask Hayley, given that Dani hadn't told her a word about what was going on.

He thought about it some more. Leo had left her because he'd fallen for someone else. Dani wanted someone who loved her.

Alex loved her.

But he hadn't actually told her that. He'd been so busy trying to keep his distance that he'd kind of assumed she'd realise how he felt about her.

Telling her now would definitely seem like too little, too late. He needed to prove to her that he loved her, and that it wasn't just because of the baby.

He needed to woo her, properly.

And he'd really have to hope that she'd give him a chance.

CHAPTER TEN

On Friday, Alex and Dani were both on a late shift. Mid-afternoon, when they were due a break, he went into the staff kitchen and to his relief found her there alone. 'Dani, can we go and talk in a quiet corner of the canteen?' he asked.

'Sorry, I'm busy,' she said.

'You're on a break,' he said, 'and it's your Year of Saying Yes, so technically you have to agree.'

'Maybe I've stopped doing that,' she said, narrowing her eyes at him.

'I wasn't trying to push you,' he said.

'No?'

'No.' He sighed. 'I was trying to make light of things and instead making a mess of it. You and I are at odds right now and we need to clear the air—if nothing else, to make things less awkward for the people who have to work with us. I'm sorry I've been such a clueless idiot, especially as you've been so brilliant with me over the last few months. Come and have a cup of tea or whatever with me, Dani. Please.'

She looked reluctant.

'Plus we need to discuss some practical things about the baby, and it ought to be sooner rather than later.'

'I guess.' She wrinkled her nose. 'All right. A cup of tea.'

'Thank you.' It was a start. And hopefully he could build on things from here and prove to her that he loved her—that he wanted to marry her for her own sake, and the words had all come out wrongly yesterday.

He found them a quiet table in the canteen.

'So what did you want to talk about?' she asked.

'We know I don't have the faulty gene, which means the baby doesn't either,' he said. 'So you don't need CVS now, and can go ahead with the dating scan as normal.'

She looked at him. 'Where exactly are you going with this?'

'I'd like to come to the scan with you,' he said.

'There's really no need. I can manage by myself.'

'I know you can manage, but it's my baby, too. And I want to be there,' he said. 'For selfish reasons. Because I'd like to see the baby's heartbeat on screen.' And to hold her hand while they looked at the screen together, though Alex judged it was probably better to keep that bit to himself for now.

'Have you told your parents the news yet?' she asked.

'About the baby?'

'About the test.'

He nodded. 'I told Mum about the results yesterday, when I came out of the counsellor's office. And I spoke to Dad this morning. I told him I'd kept the test quiet because I didn't want them having the stress of waiting for the news, but it's all good now. He said things are better between them, so I think it's finally going to be all right.'

'What about the friends you pushed away?' She paused. 'Or Lara?'

'No. But you were right yesterday. I do have a lot of bridges to rebuild.'

She lifted her chin. 'And now you know you don't have the gene, you can maybe repair your engagement.'

Was that what she really believed? That he was going to walk away from her, even though she was expecting his baby, and try to make things up with his ex? Then again, it had been almost a year since her husband had left her for someone else. Of course it would be the first thing she'd think of.

'Apart from the fact that I've heard on the grapevine Lara's seeing someone else, I'm not in love with her any more,' he said. Because he was in love with Dani—not that he thought she was ready to hear that yet. 'That's one of the other things I wanted to talk to you about. You had a late night last night, and I'm guessing you're feeling it a bit today. I'd like to keep cooking dinner for you, so you get a chance to put your feet up and rest in the evening.'

'I'd rather you didn't,' she said.

OK. He'd try another way. 'And I think we should continue our distraction list.'

She frowned. 'Why? You don't have to wait for the news any more so you don't need your mind taken off things.'

And now was the time to be honest with her. 'That's not why I want to do it,' he said. 'I enjoyed spending time with you, and I want to do more of that.'

She looked at him as if she didn't believe a single word.

'Plus, while we were doing the distraction stuff, I bought tickets for a couple of things, and it would be a pity to waste them.'

Her frown deepened. 'You didn't tell me you'd bought tickets for something.'

'I'm telling you now.'

She lifted a shoulder in a half-shrug. 'You could take someone else.'

'In theory, I could,' he said. 'But the tickets are for things I wanted to share with you.'

Her eyes filled with tears. 'Don't pretend feelings you don't have, Alex. I've been there before and I never want to be in that situation again.'

So he'd guessed right: it wasn't that she didn't have feelings for him, but that she didn't believe he had feelings for her. 'I know, and I'm not pretending anything,' he said. He looked her straight in the eye. 'I could tell you, but I don't think words are enough. You need to see it for yourself.'

She said nothing.

Then again, he didn't deserve to have this made easy for him. 'We synchronised our off duty, so I know you're not working tomorrow. I'll pick you up at one.'

'I...' She sighed. 'You're not going to give in, are you?'

'No.' Because this was way too important. He'd been an idiot and pushed her away, but he intended to fix it. He wasn't going to let her put barriers up and push him away, too.

'All right. I'll see you at one.'

'Thank you.'

Dani was ready before one o'clock the next day, knowing that Alex would be dead on time. Did he mean it about wanting to spend time with her? Or was he still thinking about things from a dutiful perspective, as the father of her baby?

For now, she'd reserve her judgement.

Alex rang her doorbell. 'OK to go?' he asked when she answered her door.

She pulled on her coat. 'Yes. Where are we going?'

'Somewhere I hope you'll like.'

Which told her nothing, but she wasn't going to argue with him. She was picking her battles carefully.

They caught the mainline train from Alexandra Palace and then the tube to Covent Garden. Alex shepherded her through the crowds and she hadn't a clue where they were going until they stopped outside the theatre and she saw the show's name all lit up: *Mamma Mia.*

'You bought tickets for this?' she asked, surprised.

He shrugged. 'It's one of your favourite musicals. Word perfect on the songs, I think you said.'

'But this isn't really your kind of music,' she said. She knew he preferred rock and blues.

'It's yours, and that's what matters,' he said.

So he really had been paying attention to some of what she'd said?

'Thank you.' But she felt really guilty when she discovered how good their seats were. Given that he could only have bought them in the last couple of weeks, he must've had to go through one of the ticket resellers to get them. She bit her lip. 'I hope you didn't pay an exorbitant price.'

'That's between me and the Internet,' he said with a smile. 'But, instead of feeling guilty, I'd rather you just bought me an ice cream in the interval. I want you to enjoy this.'

The music and dancing worked its usual magic on her, and Dani found herself holding Alex's hand in the second half of the show. She was surprised that he actually stood up with her and most of the rest of the audience for the finale and sang along to 'Mamma Mia', 'Dancing Queen' and 'Waterloo'—although he was far from word perfect, he was at least making the effort. For her? Or was she kidding herself?

'Do you have time for dinner?' he asked afterwards.

'OK, but as you bought the theatre tickets I insist on buying dinner,' she said. 'That's not negotiable.'

'All right. And thank you.'

And she didn't pull her hand away when he curled his fingers round hers and they walked back to Covent Garden.

This felt more like a real date than their 'distraction' dates ever had. So did Alex have feelings for her? Or was he still thinking mainly about the baby?

She pushed the thought away and concentrated on enjoying the Christmas lights at Covent Garden and finding somewhere to eat.

Afterwards, Alex saw her back to her flat. 'Can I see you tomorrow evening?' he asked.

She shook her head. 'Sorry. Hayley and I are watching our annual Christmas film.'

'Annual Christmas film?' he asked, looking mystified.

'Our favourite Christmas move—*Love Actually*. We watch it every year and argue over whether our favourite moment is Hugh Grant dancing or Colin Firth with his terrible Portuguese,' she explained.

'But you're free during the day?'

She shook her head. 'Sorry. I need to clean my flat and sort out my laundry.'

'Here's the deal,' he said. 'How about I do your housework in the morning, and you give me an hour and a half of your afternoon?'

He was actually offering to clean her flat for her?

She must've spoken aloud, because he smiled. 'Yes. And I'll do it the way you want me to.'

He must really want to spend time with her. 'So what does the afternoon entail?'

'Come with me and find out,' he coaxed.

And he turned out to be as good as his word, cleaning her bathroom and vacuuming her flat and even setting up her ironing board, ready to tackle her laundry pile.

'I can do my own ir—' she began.

'Yes, but you don't have to. Put your feet up and read a magazine.'

She pulled a face. 'I did enough resting when my foot was at its worst. And I feel guilty about you slaving away doing my housework.'

'There's not much difference between doing a bit of vacuuming and making dinner, you know. And you're pregnant. You need to rest.'

'Rest is a four-letter word,' she pointed out.

He sighed. 'OK. You can do your ironing.'

'Thank you.'

She'd just about finished when he said, 'It's time to go.'

Again, he wouldn't tell her what they were doing until they reached their destination: but then he ushered her into a grand London hotel.

'I thought we could have a Christmas afternoon tea,' he said.

There was a massive Christmas tree in the corner of the room, decorated with red and gold tinsel and baubles; garlands and swags in similar colours decorated the rest of the room. A pianist in the opposite corner in white tie and tails was playing a selection of Christmas songs— though not, to her relief, 'Last Christmas'.

The waiter led them over to their table, which was beautifully set with a white damask tablecloth, bone china cups and saucers, and a real silver tea strainer. Once they'd chosen their tea—English breakfast for Alex and passionfruit and orange for Dani—the waiter brought over a china cake stand with their afternoon tea. 'The sandwiches on the bottom tier are cream cheese and cucumber, turkey and cranberry, and ham and mustard,' he said. 'The middle layer are warm winter spiced scones, wrapped in a napkin to keep them warm, with apricot jam and clotted cream; and on the top there are apple and cinnamon doughnut baubles, mini mince pies, Stollen bites and mini chocolate Yule logs. If there's anything you need, just ask.'

'Thank you,' Alex said.

'This is lovely,' Dani said. It was the sort of thing she would've enjoyed planning as a surprise treat; and it was wonderful to be on the receiving end.

'It's meant to be one of the the best Christmas afternoon teas in London,' he said.

'I can see why. The bread's perfect,' she said after her first taste of the turkey and cranberry sandwich.

And the scones were even nicer. 'Best ever. I'm definitely going to bring my parents here,' she said. 'My mum would love this.'

'Have you told your parents about the baby?' he asked.

'Not yet,' she said. 'It's something I'd rather do face to face.' She looked at him. 'Have you told yours?'

'I'm holding out until we have a scan photo,' he said.

'That's a good idea. I might do the same.'

'Do you want me to come with you when you tell them?' he asked.

That rather depended on how things were between

them. 'Maybe,' she hedged. And should she offer to go with him? But that assumed a level in their relationship that she wasn't sure they'd reached.

'Just let me know. I'll leave it to you,' he said.

So he wasn't being pushy about it. That made her feel a little bit better.

Even so she was quiet when she went over to Hayley's for their planned movie evening. How were she and Alex going to tell people about the baby? And how were people going to react?

'Are you all right?' Hayley asked when she handed Dani a mug of hot chocolate.

'Sure,' Dani fibbed. 'We're really busy at work. You know how it is.'

'You would tell me if something was wrong, wouldn't you?'

Guilt flooded through her. 'Of course,' she said. Nothing was wrong, now—Alex's test results meant that the baby definitely didn't have Huntington's. But if she told Hayley about the situation tonight, she knew her best friend would worry about her, and she wanted Hayley to enjoy her wedding to the full. Dani promised herself that she'd tell Hayley everything when she was back from her honeymoon.

Though she found herself feeling more wistful than usual when they watched the film. The endings of some of the relationships in the story were clearly happy, and others were more ambiguous. How would it all work out between Alex and herself? She still didn't have a clue how he felt towards her, even though he'd spent the weekend making such a huge fuss of her. Was it only because of the baby, or was it for her?

* * *

Alex walked into the pub and scanned the room for his best friend. Tom had clearly been watching the doors because he raised his hand from his seat by the bar. Funny, he didn't look any different from when Alex had last seen him, the best part of a year ago. And yet so much had changed in that time.

'Thanks for meeting me tonight,' Alex said when he reached Tom's table. 'Especially as I didn't exactly give you a lot of notice and it's coming up to Christmas.' And especially as he'd been totally unavailable for the last ten months.

'It wasn't that hard to move things round. And it's good to see you, Alex. I've missed you.' Tom gave him a hug. 'So how's it going?'

'It's a bit complicated,' Alex said ruefully. 'Let me buy you another pint and I'll tell you about it.'

When he sat back down at their table, Tom said, 'Explain complicated.'

'Put it this way—how would you feel about being my best man and godfather?' Alex asked.

Tom stared at him, looking shocked. 'Wait, what? Marriage and a baby? When did all this happen?'

Alex filled him in on how Dani had rescued him when he'd been at his lowest point, her unexpected pregnancy, and the fact that she'd just refused to marry him. 'Which was all my fault for not asking her properly,' he admitted. 'I just said to her that we could get married.'

'You said what? You idiot! Why didn't you tell her you were madly in love with her and she'd make you the happiest man in the world if she'd agree to marry you?' Tom shook his head sorrowfully. 'Alex, I'm beginning to think you shouldn't be allowed out without your own personal PR person to tell you what to actually say, and also tell you when to shut up.'

'I could probably do with some personal skills training,' Alex admitted.

'Book a course online. Tonight,' Tom said, rolling his eyes. 'So what happens now?'

'I'm trying to show her that I love her,' Alex said. 'Because I keep getting it wrong when I open my mouth, and actions speak louder than words, right?'

'That depends on what you do,' Tom said.

'If I *can* persuade her to marry me, would you be my best man—and godfather to our baby?' Alex asked.

'I'd be honoured. But only if I meet her first and she actually likes me,' Tom warned.

'Don't you need to see if you like her, too?' Alex asked.

'From what you've told me,' Tom said, 'I already like her. She's good for you.' He paused. 'Have your parents met her yet?'

'No. And I haven't told them about the baby either.'

Tom groaned. 'You really do like living dangerously, don't you?'

'She hasn't told her parents either,' Alex pointed out. 'We've been waiting on the results of my genetic test. Once we've had the dating scan and got photographs for them, we're going to come clean.' He dragged in a breath. 'And I'm pretty sure they're all going to want to know what we're going to do—if we're going to raise the baby together as a family.'

'Is that what you both want?' Tom asked.

'It's what I want. What I hope Dani wants,' Alex said.

'But until I can convince her how I feel about her, I need to keep everything under wraps. Just for a little bit longer.'

'Good luck,' Tom said, 'because I think you're going to need it.'

On the Monday Dani was able to book a scan for the end of the following week. Alex continued to spend the evenings with her, cooking dinner while she had a power nap, and she had to admit that she really appreciated the rest—the hormones were really wiping her out.

He also took her to a candlelit carol service in the middle of the week. Singing Victorian carols in an ancient church was incredibly moving; and it felt natural for Dani to tighten her fingers round his when he held her hand. Afterwards, they walked through Trafalgar Square to get hot chocolate and see the Christmas tree, still hand in hand.

This felt like the way things had been when they'd first started their 'distraction' dates, she thought. Though he still hadn't kissed her or said anything about his feelings. She had absolutely no idea where she stood with him. He must care about her, or he wouldn't be trying to look after her; then again, was he only doing that because she was pregnant and he felt it was his duty to look after her?

Normally, she would've been straight-talking and asked. But they were heading towards Christmas—and last year her world had imploded at Christmas. She really couldn't face a repeat of that.

At the weekend, Alex produced tickets for the Christmas trail at Kew. 'It's meant to be really gorgeous,' he said. 'Everything from a tunnel of lights through to the light show at the Palm House.'

And the trail lived up to the hype, with festive lights and sculptures everywhere. There were old-fashioned fairground rides; although Alex refused to let her go on the helter-skelter, citing her newly healed foot, he agreed to ride with her on the old-fashioned carousel. Dani felt ever so slightly swept off her feet when he helped her onto the white horse with its gold-painted mane; and she liked the fact that, as the horses seated two, Alex climbed on behind her and wrapped his arms round her waist.

Tonight he was making her feel really cherished.

There were fire pits next to stalls of gourmet marsh-mallows; she picked cinnamon and apple flavour, and Alex toasted them for her.

'This is amazing,' she said. 'I've never done this be-fore.'

'Me, neither,' he said. He gestured to the children hold-ing their parents' hands as they queued up to see Father Christmas. 'This could be us in a few years, bringing our little one.'

So was this thing between them still all about the baby? Or was it about them?

She still didn't have an answer by the end of the eve-ning, even though Alex actually kissed her goodnight, and it made her feel weak at the knees.

Was she getting carried away by the magic of Christ-mas? Or did they have a future?

The day before Dani's scan appointment, the ultrasound department called her.

'I'm so sorry. The radiographer you're booked in with has gone down with the virus that's doing the rounds, so I'm afraid we'll have to reschedule your scan appoint-ment,' the receptionist told her.

'Thanks for letting me know.' Dani was able to re-book the appointment for just after Christmas, but there was a hard knot of disappointment in her stomach. She'd hoped that going to the scan would finally push Alex into talking about his feelings. It looked as if she was going to have to wait.

She told him about the change that evening when he'd cooked them pasta and garlic bread at his place. 'So it'll be another couple of weeks.'

'Are you OK with that?'

She shrugged. 'You know what it's like, working in a hospital over the winter. People go down with viruses all over the place. It can't be helped.'

But the disappointment must have shown on her face, because he wrapped his arms round her. 'So this means either telling your parents without the photograph or wait-ing a few more days.'

'I'd rather give them a photograph,' she said.

'OK. I'll go with that, too,' he said.

But he still didn't tell her he loved her.

Then again, she hadn't told him either.

One of them was going to have to say it first. But right now she didn't want to take the risk, in case she was guessing wrongly and he didn't say it back.

On Christmas Eve, Hayley and Sam got married. Dani, as the bridesmaid, couldn't help being slightly teary-eyed as they made their vows; it was good to see them both looking so happy. And it gave her so much hope for the future; last Christmas Eve, she'd felt that love had just stopped existing. This year, it would be different.

She loved the way that Sam's brother had organised a snow machine for the photographs. This was what a real wedding should be like, she thought: full of light and love and laughter.

Alex turned up as one of the evening guests, looking handsome in a formal suit. How ridiculous that it should make her heart skip a beat; she saw him in a suit all the time at work. And yet when he came over to talk to her, her knees went weak. The way he smiled at her, the warmth in his eyes… Was she getting carried away with the wedding atmosphere, or did it mean something?

'You look amazing,' he said. 'That dress really suits you.'

And, being empire line, it hid the fact that she was starting to develop the tiniest, tiniest bump.

'Thank you.' She smiled at him.

'Dance with me?'

She nodded, and of course Maybe Baby would choose that exact moment to play a slower song. What could she do but step forward into his arms and sway with him to the music?

I love you.

Alex almost said the words.

Almost.

But this was Christmas Eve. The first anniversary of the day that Dani's husband had broken her heart. This would be the worst possible time for him to talk about love. And it wasn't the right place either: her best friend's wedding.

So he just held her close and hoped that he'd find the right words to tell her, and the right place to say the words.

Soon.

CHAPTER ELEVEN

On Christmas Day, Dani drove over to her parents' house.

Mandy Owens greeted her with a hug. 'I'm so glad you're home. I mean, after la—' She stopped mid-word, looking horrified.

Dani knew what her mother had just stopped herself saying. 'Mum, honestly, it's OK. You don't have to walk on eggshells or worry about what you say because of what happened last Christmas with Leo. It's a year ago now and I'm fine. I'm over him.' And, thanks to Alex, she really was.

'I just worry about you being lonely, love.'

Dani smiled. 'I'm way too busy to be lonely, Mum.' This time next year, she'd be busier still. Not that she could talk about that yet. So instead, after they'd exchanged presents, she distracted her mum with the shots of Hayley's wedding on her phone.

'And you say she's gone to Iceland for her honeymoon?' Mandy asked.

Dani nodded. 'How romantic is that? Christmas, the Northern Lights, and guaranteed snow.'

And although she really enjoyed spending the day with her family, with the chatter and the board games and their traditional post-lunch walk in the park, she realised as she drove home that she'd actually missed being with Alex.

Did he feel the same way about her?

Maybe it was time she stopped being such a coward and actually asked him.

She'd do it at the scan, she decided.

As she walked through her front door, her phone pinged to signal an incoming message. She looked at the screen, half expecting it to be a late one from Hayley, but it was from Alex.

Merry Christmas.

So he had been thinking about her, then.

Merry Christmas, she texted back. How was your day?

She knew that, like her, he'd spent his day with his parents.

Good. Yours?

Good, she replied.

I'm glad. See you at the scan on Tuesday?

The scan. She wasn't sure if she was more excited or terrified about it. Everything had been on hold for so long. Would the scan finally be the place where they could move on?

See you Tuesday, she typed.

On Tuesday morning, Dani met Alex in the hospital reception area at half-past eight.

'Given that the most of the radiography department

know both of us, even though we can insist on patient confidentiality,' she said, 'this is when I think we're going to be outed.'

'Would you rather say that I'm just supporting you as your colleague?' he asked.

She damped down the hurt that he'd even asked. 'If you like,' she said, keeping her voice cool.

'Actually, I don't like. At all,' he said. 'I'm going with you because this is my baby.'

'So people are going to know. They're going to ask questions.'

'Bring it on,' he said.

The radiographer called Dani in to the ultrasound suite. 'Dani, it *is* you!'

'Hi, Jessie,' Dani said with a smile.

'I wondered if it was when I saw your name on the list, but then I thought it was probably just someone else with the same name,' Jessie said. 'I had no idea you were expecting.' She looked at Alex and raised her eyebrows. 'OK. Obviously I'll keep full patient confidentiality.'

'Thank you,' he said.

Jessie looked at Dani's notes. 'So you're almost fourteen weeks.'

'I know it's really late for a dating scan,' Dani said, 'but we had a very good reason for leaving it this long.'

'My biological father died from Huntington's,' Alex said, 'and we didn't know if I'd inherited it. We had to wait for my test results to come through to see if we needed to consider CVS for the baby.'

'I assume that your test was all clear, then?' Jessie asked.

'Thankfully, yes,' Alex replied.

'That's good,' Jessie said. 'One less complication to

worry about. Well, not that I'd dare try to tell an obstetric consultant and a registrar about when to worry in pregnancy!'

'I did have a scan booked for twelve weeks, but the radiographer I was booked in with went down with that virus that was doing the rounds, and then it was Christmas,' Dani said.

'Well, you're here now and that's what matters,' Jessie said. 'I guess you already know the drill, as you both use the portable scanners in your department or the emergency department, but do either of you have any questions about the procedure?'

Dani shook her head. 'No questions. We just want to see the baby.'

'It's always a lovely moment, seeing a baby on the screen,' Jessie said. 'But when it's your own it's very different. If you didn't bring tissues, I have some.' She gestured to the box by the side of the low bed where Dani was lying. 'I'm warning you now that you'll need them.' She looked at Alex. 'And I mean *both* of you.'

'Thanks,' Dani said.

She bared her stomach and Jessie smoothed radioconductive gel over her skin, then ran the head of the transceiver across Dani's abdomen.

'And here we are,' Jessie said quietly, turning the screen so they could both see it. 'One baby. There's a nice heartbeat there; I can see ten fingers and ten toes, and the spine looks good.' She did some quick measurements. 'And you're spot on with dates, Dani. The baby's measuring at fourteen weeks.'

Dani could barely take it in; her whole attention was focused on the black and white image on the screen, the heart beating steadily and the baby moving around in the womb.

She'd seen babies plenty of times before on the screen when she'd performed an emergency scan. But Jessie was right: although it was always a lovely moment to see the baby's heart beating, it was completely different when it was your own baby. Visceral. And she was shocked by the tide of fierce, protective love that swept over her.

She glanced up at Alex and realised that his eyes were wet.

So were her own. She hadn't even realised that she was crying.

'I'll give you both a moment,' Jessie said, and left the ultrasound suite.

'Our baby.' Alex's eyes were wide with wonder. 'Dani. There's something I want to say to you.'

'Me first,' she said. Because now was the time to be brave. 'I've realised over the past couple of months that you're not very good with emotional stuff. When you just casually said we could get married, it sounded as if you'd sort of proposed out of duty—that you thought you ought to do it for the baby's sake. But the way you've been with me ever since... It makes me think—hope—that you might feel about me the same way that I feel about you.'

'I hope you feel the same way about me,' he said, 'because I love you, Dani. I know our relationship has been totally upside down, with the baby coming first, and I was trying to hold back because I didn't want to be a burden to you if I ended up testing positive for Huntington's. But then you were so tired, and I wanted to support you, and I found myself falling for you anyway. When we started dating, even though we called it distracting each other from waiting for the test results, I fell for you even more. And I made a complete mess of asking you to marry me. It was too late to tell you then that I loved you because it seemed like an afterthought—and it wasn't, Dani.' He shook his head in apparent frustration. 'It's so stupid how I always know the right thing to say at work, but when it comes to my personal life I make such a hash of it.'

'But then you tried to show me how you felt,' she said. 'You did some really special things for me—that carol concert, taking me to *Mamma Mia*, and toasting marshmallows for me at Kew. It showed me you'd listened to what I said.' She paused. 'I thought you might say something at Hayley's wedding.'

'I wanted to,' he admitted. 'But it was Christmas Eve, the anniversary of a really bad time in your life. Part of me wanted to say something to make you forget that, but part of me didn't want to risk the association.'

'Actually, you were right not to say anything,' she said. 'Christmas Eve wasn't appropriate.'

He dropped down on one knee. 'This probably isn't an appropriate time either—and my best friend says I need my own PR person to tell me when to speak and what to say—but I love you, Dani, and you'd make me the happiest man in the world if you'd agree to marry me.' He took a deep breath. 'Danielle Owens, you make my world a better, brighter place, and I want to spend the rest of my life with you. Make a real family with you. Will you marry me?'

She took his hand and drew him up to his feet. 'I love you, too, Alex. Yes.'

He kissed her then, and it was so tender that she found herself in tears all over again.

'Hey.' He kissed her tears away.

'They're happy tears,' she said.

'Good.' He wrapped his arms round her and kissed her again. 'So how fast do you reckon we can organise an engagement party?'

'That's an easy one,' she said. 'We have New Year coming up. Your flat's bigger than mine. All we need to sort out are drinks and nibbles—which we can buy ready-made from the supermarket—and a playlist of music.'

'What, no pomegranate molasses?' he teased.

She laughed. 'We're going to do something uncomplicated for once.'

'Sounds good to me.' He looked at her. 'So we need to tell our parents. And Hayley and Sam.' He paused. 'Um. I'm assuming Hayley will be your bridesmaid and godmother?'

'If that's all right with you.'

'I'm more than happy.'

'What about your best friend?' she asked. 'Have you started patching things up yet?'

He nodded. 'We've started rebuilding bridges.'

'So I'm guessing he'd be your best man and our baby's godfather?'

'If you're happy with that.'

She smiled. 'I'm happy.'

Jessie knocked on the door and came back in. 'All OK?' she asked.

'All very OK,' Alex and Dani said in unison.

'Excellent. I forgot to ask you—would you like a photograph, and if so how many copies?'

'Six,' she said promptly. 'One each for us, one for both sets of parents, and two for the godparents.'

'And we have an engagement party, a wedding and a christening to plan,' Alex said, holding Dani close. 'This time, we're going to try to get things the right way round...'

EPILOGUE

July

'THIS HAS TO be the most beautiful baby in the history of the universe,' Mandy Owens said, giving her new grandson one last kiss before passing him to Tracey Morgan for a cuddle.

'He's adorable,' Tracey agreed. 'And my daughter-in-law is the cleverest girl in the world.'

Alex and Dani exchanged a glance. Their parents had definitely forgiven them for sitting on the news for the first few months. Mandy had cried when they'd given her a copy of the scan photo, and Sid had then grilled Alex to within an inch of his life, making absolutely sure that Alex wasn't going to hurt Dani the way that Leo had.

Tracey had cried, too, and hugged Dani. 'It's because of you that we have our son back—and now a grandchild to look forward to as well. No more shadows.'

'At the beginning of last year, I think the world was a difficult place for all of us,' Mandy said. 'But now the sun's shining, our kids are happy, and we've got little Harry William Sidney Morgan to look forward to making a fuss over.'

'What, even when his nappy needs changing?' Alex asked with a grin.

'I have a feeling that's going to be our department, Will,' Sid Owens said with a rueful smile.

'Of course it is,' Will Morgan agreed. 'We're modern granddads. And the nappies nowadays are much easier to sort out than they were when our two were young.'

'Unlike the prams,' Sid said, looking mock-disgusted.

Alex laughed. 'I happen to know how much time you two spent researching the best car seat that turns into a buggy and a pram. You loved every second of playing with it in the shop. And I hate to think what his wooden train set's going to be like when he's older.'

'As if we're plotting how many bridges, turntables and sheds we're going to have,' Will teased, and hugged Dani. 'I'm so thrilled and honoured you named him after both his granddads.'

'Seconded,' Sid said.

'Just as, if we have a girl next time, her middle names will be Amanda and Tracey,' Dani said with a smile.

Her mother and Alex's both went pink with pleasure.

'I can't wait to take him to the park,' Will said.

'We need one with a boating lake,' Sid said, tapping the side of his nose.

'And an area where we can launch a rocket—not one of those foot-pump air things but the proper sort with a motor and a parachute,' Will added.

Alex and Dani exchanged a glance, not sure which made them happier—the fact that their parents all got on well, or the way their fathers were having such fun plotting what they wanted to do with their grandson.

Just then, there was a knock at the door.

'Come in,' Dani said. 'Save us from the granddads and their trains, boats and rockets.'

Hayley and Sam walked in, carrying a bottle of champagne, some plastic glasses and a card. 'Congratulations,' Hayley said, and handed the bottle and glasses to Danielle's father. 'Sid, would you and Will mind...?'

'Of course,' Sid said, and he and Will sorted out the cork and pouring a glass for everyone.

'And once I get a cuddle with my newborn godson,' Hayley added, 'I might just forgive you for originally keeping the news from me for so long, Danielle Morgan.'

Tracey handed the baby to her with a smile. 'He's so like Alex when he was born, Hayley, though I know his eyes will change and be like Dani's.'

'Oh, he's beautiful. Well, little man, welcome to the world.' Hayley cuddled him. 'And, unlike your mum, I don't sit on exciting news for months instead of telling my best friend who's actually more like a sister than a friend. So you can gurgle at your mum and tell her that at Christmas, young Harry, you're going to have a little playmate.'

'Wait—what?' Dani asked. 'You and Sam...?'

'We're three months. I was going to tell you earlier,' Hayley said, beaming, 'except we were a teensy bit busy planning a wedding.'

Will gave her a hug and clapped Sam on the shoulder. 'That was Dani's line when we told you, Haze, and you said that was even more nonsense than waiting until you're past the first trimester to tell the people closest to you. And, as an obstetrician, I might remind you that I'm good at doing maths and counting backwards.'

'OK, so I waited until the first trimester was over.

Next time, we tell each other the second we've done the test,' Hayley said.

'It's a deal.' Dani hugged her. 'Congratulations, both of you.'

'Thanks.' Sam smiled at her and took the baby from his wife. 'Hello, gorgeous Harry. And don't listen to your mum about trains, boats and rockets. They're great. Your dad and I are going to be right there with you and the granddads. And we're going to teach you and the Bump how to rock-climb and skate and bungee-jump...'

He was greeted with a round of groans from the four women.

'It could be worse,' Alex pointed out. 'Mum, Mandy— has he shown you that video of people doing the forward abseiling?'

'Nightmare,' Dani said. 'Don't even think about scaring them, Sam. We'll stick to skating and trains, OK?'

Sam kissed the baby. 'Your mum's scary. I'd better do what she says. And give you back to your dad, because I think there's a nappy change needed.'

'That would be perfect practice for December,' Dani said with a wink.

'She's right,' Hayley agreed. 'Plus it's godfather duties.'

Sam groaned and accepted a nappy from Alex. 'I can't even claim that I have to get back to work instead, because we came up at the end of our shift.' Deftly, he changed the nappy. 'Right, Harry. Now you smell nice again, you can go back to your mum.'

He handed the baby back to Dani, and accepted a glass of champagne from Will.

'Welcome to Harry,' Alex said, lifting up his glass.

'And congratulations to Hayley and Sam—because babies are the most precious gift of all.'

'The most precious gift of all,' everyone echoed, and lifted their glasses.

* * * * *

If you missed the previous story in the
MIRACLES AT MUSWELL HILL HOSPITAL
duet look out for

CHRISTMAS WITH HER DAREDEVIL DOC

*If you enjoyed this story, check out
these other great reads from
Kate Hardy*

*MUMMY, NURSE...DUCHESS?
THE MIDWIFE'S PREGNANCY MIRACLE
CAPTURING THE SINGLE DAD'S HEART
HER PLAYBOY'S PROPOSAL*

All available now!

MILLS & BOON®
Hardback – November 2017

ROMANCE

The Italian's Christmas Secret	Sharon Kendrick
A Diamond for the Sheikh's Mistress	Abby Green
The Sultan Demands His Heir	Maya Blake
Claiming His Scandalous Love-Child	Julia James
Valdez's Bartered Bride	Rachael Thomas
The Greek's Forbidden Princess	Annie West
Kidnapped for the Tycoon's Baby	Louise Fuller
A Night, A Consequence, A Vow	Angela Bissell
Christmas with Her Millionaire Boss	Barbara Wallace
Snowbound with an Heiress	Jennifer Faye
Newborn Under the Christmas Tree	Sophie Pembroke
His Mistletoe Proposal	Christy McKellen
The Spanish Duke's Holiday Proposal	Robin Gianna
The Rescue Doc's Christmas Miracle	Amalie Berlin
Christmas with Her Daredevil Doc	Kate Hardy
Their Pregnancy Gift	Kate Hardy
A Family Made at Christmas	Scarlet Wilson
Their Mistletoe Baby	Karin Baine
The Texan Takes a Wife	Charlene Sands
Twins for the Billionaire	Sarah M. Anderson

MILLS & BOON®
Large Print – November 2017

ROMANCE

The Pregnant Kavakos Bride	Sharon Kendrick
The Billionaire's Secret Princess	Caitlin Crews
Sicilian's Baby of Shame	Carol Marinelli
The Secret Kept from the Greek	Susan Stephens
A Ring to Secure His Crown	Kim Lawrence
Wedding Night with Her Enemy	Melanie Milburne
Salazar's One-Night Heir	Jennifer Hayward
The Mysterious Italian Houseguest	Scarlet Wilson
Bound to Her Greek Billionaire	Rebecca Winters
Their Baby Surprise	Katrina Cudmore
The Marriage of Inconvenience	Nina Singh

HISTORICAL

Ruined by the Reckless Viscount	Sophia James
Cinderella and the Duke	Janice Preston
A Warriner to Rescue Her	Virginia Heath
Forbidden Night with the Warrior	Michelle Willingham
The Foundling Bride	Helen Dickson

MEDICAL

Mummy, Nurse...Duchess?	Kate Hardy
Falling for the Foster Mum	Karin Baine
The Doctor and the Princess	Scarlet Wilson
Miracle for the Neurosurgeon	Lynne Marshall
English Rose for the Sicilian Doc	Annie Claydon
Engaged to the Doctor Sheikh	Meredith Webber

MILLS & BOON®
Hardback – December 2017

ROMANCE

His Queen by Desert Decree	Lynne Graham
A Christmas Bride for the King	Abby Green
Captive for the Sheikh's Pleasure	Carol Marinelli
Legacy of His Revenge	Cathy Williams
A Night of Royal Consequences	Susan Stephens
Carrying His Scandalous Heir	Julia James
Christmas at the Tycoon's Command	Jennifer Hayward
Innocent in the Billionaire's Bed	Clare Connelly
Snowed in with the Reluctant Tycoon	Nina Singh
The Magnate's Holiday Proposal	Rebecca Winters
The Billionaire's Christmas Baby	Marion Lennox
Christmas Bride for the Boss	Kate Hardy
Christmas with the Best Man	Susan Carlisle
Navy Doc on Her Christmas List	Amy Ruttan
Christmas Bride for the Sheikh	Carol Marinelli
Her Knight Under the Mistletoe	Annie O'Neil
The Nurse's Special Delivery	Louisa George
Her New Year Baby Surprise	Sue MacKay
His Secret Son	Brenda Jackson
Best Man Under the Mistletoe	Jules Bennett

MILLS & BOON®
Large Print – November 2017

ROMANCE

An Heir Made in the Marriage Bed	Anne Mather
The Prince's Stolen Virgin	Maisey Yates
Protecting His Defiant Innocent	Michelle Smart
Pregnant at Acosta's Demand	Maya Blake
The Secret He Must Claim	Chantelle Shaw
Carrying the Spaniard's Child	Jennie Lucas
A Ring for the Greek's Baby	Melanie Milburne
The Runaway Bride and the Billionaire	Kate Hardy
The Boss's Fake Fiancée	Susan Meier
The Millionaire's Redemption	Therese Beharrie
Captivated by the Enigmatic Tycoon	Bella Bucannon

HISTORICAL

Marrying His Cinderella Countess	Louise Allen
A Ring for the Pregnant Debutante	Laura Martin
The Governess Heiress	Elizabeth Beacon
The Warrior's Damsel in Distress	Meriel Fuller
The Knight's Scarred Maiden	Nicole Locke

MEDICAL

Healing the Sheikh's Heart	Annie O'Neil
A Life-Saving Reunion	Alison Roberts
The Surgeon's Cinderella	Susan Carlisle
Saved by Doctor Dreamy	Dianne Drake
Pregnant with the Boss's Baby	Sue MacKay
Reunited with His Runaway Doc	Lucy Clark

MILLS & BOON®

Why shop at millsandboon.co.uk?

Each year, thousands of romance readers find their perfect read at millsandboon.co.uk. That's because we're passionate about bringing you the very best romantic fiction. Here are some of the advantages of shopping at www.millsandboon.co.uk:

* **Get new books first**—you'll be able to buy your favourite books one month before they hit the shops

* **Get exclusive discounts**—you'll also be able to buy our specially created monthly collections, with up to 50% off the RRP

* **Find your favourite authors**—latest news, interviews and new releases for all your favourite authors and series on our website, plus ideas for what to try next

* **Join in**—once you've bought your favourite books, don't forget to register with us to rate, review and join in the discussions

Visit **www.millsandboon.co.uk** for all this and more today!